In memory of Vera Hughes (1920-2005)

A true teacher

Thunder, Third Apparition, a child crowned, with a tree in his hand.

Macbeth:

What is this,

That rises like the issue of a king;

And wears upon his baby brow the round

And top of sovereignty?

All:

Listen, but speak not to't.

****

Shakespeare, *Macbeth*.

I

I bombed down the corridor, yanked open the door and bounded into the kitchen. Lolek, thank Christ, was there, stacking up the pots and pans. He had the radio on again. That '80s station again. Every night was '80s night in Lolek's kitchen:

When the river was deep, I didn't falter,
When the mountain was high, I still believed,
When the valley was low, it didn't stop me, oh no,

He turned his plump, kind face to me and smiled. 'Ah, Miss Julie, how good to see you.'

'The key, Lolek, the key.'

I knew you were waiting, 'Knew you were waiting for me.

'But, Miss Julie.' He shrugged, then stretched out his arms, eyes dancing with laughter. I flung down my sports bag, grabbed the radio and launched it against the wall. KERPOW! It shattered into a gazillion splintering shards. The dancing stopped. The laughter stopped. I reached across to the worktop, picked up a breadknife and pointed it at his chest.

'The chapel key, Lolek. The dining room door. Now.'

'But, Miss Julie, it is forbidden. I cannot give you this one. Caesar has warned us.'

I looked at Lolek, Lolek looked at me, and I knew I could still back out if I wanted to, passing it off as a game or another slice of Constantine's Chambers theatrics. I was, after all, wearing a white cotton tunic, tied with a grey twine belt and emblazoned with a purple diamond on the front. I had silver-buckled shoes on my feet and a scarlet bandana, to top it all off, twizzled through my jet-black hair.

I could easily have backed out. Maybe I should have. But I took Macbeth's advice instead. To return would indeed be as 'tedious as go o'er'. And besides, Caesar had already given me my mission. I had to rescue the Grail.

So, I stepped forward with the knife…

And here I am, still in my tunic, but minus bandana, belt and shoes. This is where the Grail has led me. This is where all the stories have led me – from Shakespeare to King Arthur to the gods and goddesses of ancient Ireland – from Dad to Mr. Martin to Caesar himself – this dark, cold dungeon that could be a prison, could be a hospital, could be a torture chamber for all I know.

The bed's all hard and lumpy. I pull the grey and white sheet up tight. It's night outside. An iron grille masks the tiny slit of window high on the wall to my right. I can see the outline of a door in front of me, but no light, only dark. I want a ciggie. My head hurts. My chest hurts. Everything hurts.

So, do I regret it all then? Coming to Constantine's Chambers, I mean. I could, so Dr. Tenby said, have had my pick of any Uni in the country. But even if that was true (which I doubt), it's been well and truly kaiboshed now. All I can do, in the time I've got left, is tell this story. And I will. I'll make a proper fist of it. And anyway, at least I went down fighting. Macbeth'd be proud. Caesar, I know, *is* proud. *And* I saw a vision. We *both* saw a vision. Jacqueline and me. A cast-iron, copper-bottomed, rock-solid vision. She can't say it didn't happen. Can't say it wasn't real. Whatever pans out now, or whether she's dead or alive, we'll always have that. Our secret forever.

Lolek chucked me the key. I put the knife down. The doorbell rang twice – beeeep beeeep – then BANG BANG BANG at the outer door. 'Leg it, Lolek. Any way you can. Climb out the window.' I looked around – stupidly – like I might find his wife hiding in the dishwasher.

'Where's Glinka?'

'Tesco, Miss Julie.'

'Good.'

I grabbed my sports bag and ran, through the blacked-out dining room, across the threshold and down the steps, three at a time to the chapel. At the bottom I stopped stone dead. Caesar was standing at the altar in a purple robe with white trimmings at the neck and cuffs. A golden circlet ran through his bushy brown hair. He looked me in the eye, I looked at him back, and the Grail was a silver blur, as he lifted it high above his head ...

II

I wasn't always this way, you know. In the beginning, I had no need for stories. I lived in the Garden of Eden. Absence, loss and lack were words without meaning. I scrunch up my eyes, desperate to get back, and see a huge, colossal sun, five or six times its usual size, high in the East, higher than the tree-tops of Falkner Square Gardens, illuminating and making holy my childhood paradise.

I was fourteen when the shadow came, and Dad – Michael Cornelius Carlton – saved me with his stories. Dad – God rest him – was a storyteller and a bard, and that's where it comes from. He was a tall, slim, round-faced fella with a mop of prematurely white hair, as white as mine and Vivi's were black. He loved to talk and tell tall tales, winking and smiling at all and sundry, from Simon, the surly postman, to Adam and Cecylia, our studious Polish lodgers. He was from Mayo, in the far west of Ireland. His laughter, wild and free, echoed and rang (together with a never-ending stream of 80s pop) through every nook and cranny of the house.

Where Dad was outgoing and exuberant, Ma (God rest her too) was cautious and watchful. She was Irish as well – from Cork – but that was where the parallels ended. Ma was small like a bird; practical and focused. She had to be, I suppose. It can't have been easy, keeping all the plates spinning, juggling the round of cooking, cleaning and washing with her job at that care home in Wavertree.

As I got older, I started to sense a bit of strain. Sometimes, for instance, when doing the dishes, Ma'd sweat buckets and the kitchen would smell. I used to stand at the door, dying to dash in and wrap my arms around her, scared off though by the brown strands of hair glued to her forehead. Our Old Man was an old-school bloke in many respects. He took no part in household chores. It was Vivi, nine times out of ten, who gave Ma the hand she needed.

'Vivi', by the way, is short for Genevieve. I'm the only one who calls her that. I don't know why. It just sounds nice – poetic and musical. Her friends call her Jenny or Jen, but the other day at Lime Street she told me she's always liked Vivi best. I didn't say anything, but it meant the world to me what she said.

Vivi is five years older and five inches taller than me, her figure somehow both fuller and slimmer than mine. Her hair, until recently, flowed down in streaming, luscious waves in lustrous contrast with my sleek and glossy sheen.

Speaking of hair, you'll see me now and again with a little ponytail at the nape of the neck, but nine times out of ten I go for the messy bob (with a sweep from left to right) that frames my face so well. I've Dad's moonface, you see, while Vivi's squared-off chin and jutting cheekbones form a glamourous (if slightly irregular) oval. She looks nothing like Dad or Ma, and the only feature she shares with me is her sparkly brown eyes, wide and round like saucers.

Our house, half-way along Canning Street, has two bay windows and a petrel blue door. It's still the same. We've spent the last two weeks there, Vivi and me.

Plonked on the orange rug, by the front room window, for years and years, was our beloved box of hand-me-downs. One night, when I was about seven or eight, Dad came back from work holding a banana crate. He took it upstairs and next morning there it was on the rug, jam-packed with costumes of a million different sizes, shapes and colours. Neither of us thought to ask where the clothes had come from. There were hats, dresses, scarves, gowns and robes as well as the red bandana Vivi said made me look like a pirate smuggling treasure into some moonlit cave. I liked that image. But I liked the pearly necklaces at the bottom of the crate as well. We could pretend to be proper grown-ups with them – glamourous ladies stepping out into the city and the night.

That city was Liverpool. As a kid I found it both beautiful and terrifying, with its pinnacles and domes and all those red-faced men and women shouting and singing on its narrow streets. Dad worked as a conductor at Lime Street. Now and again he would spirit me off to the station, smuggle me into the cab and whisk me away to places with fancy names like Chester, Crewe and Manchester Airport. But such ventures were rare. My world began and ended (apart from the occasional holiday in Southport or Llandudno) with Falkner Square Gardens at one end of the street and the big brown tower of the Anglican Cathedral at the other.

That tower set its mark on me from the start. I liked its solidity. It was sturdy and wide as well as dreamy and high. I felt I could rely on it. It wouldn't let me down. It was a Guardian Angel, keeping tabs on myself, my family and all the little streets, houses and squares that made up Liverpool 8. Nothing bad could happen, I said to myself, as long as the tower was there. If I leant out far enough from my bedroom window and turned my head to the right, it would be there for me at any time of day or night. That, I honestly believed, was the most fantastic, fabulous miracle in the whole wide world.

Downstairs in the hall, reclining against the bannister was the red hoop, my favourite toy. I'd dash out down the steps with it, rolling it beside me as I walked, then pushing it ahead as I started to run – faster and faster – across Bedford Street and Catharine Street, down and around onto Little Saint Bride Street, then left onto Hope Street – the tower watching on from the other side – then left again onto Huskie, around the top of the Square and into the heart of the Gardens.

Grand Georgian terraces, stylish and shabby at the same time, surrounded me. Closer in, a ring of poplars kept guard, then, closer still, the golden tips, like spear-points, of the black iron fence circling the park.

Up and up I threw the hoop, high into the sky. Hanging for an eternity, then looping around in a figure of eight, it dropped down slowly at first, then quicker and quicker, dive-bombing the dark-haired girl below. I closed my eyes, stretched out my arm and caught the hoop, easy peasy every time. I shut my eyes because I knew that I'd catch it. My faith was absolute. Not once did I drop it.

My childhood had two ends, not one. I was just gone fourteen, as I said before. My birthday's on September 21st and it was either the 28th or 29th when the shadow came and finished things off. It was a dull afternoon. I was standing in my room after school in my grey and maroon uniform. The bedclothes were a rumpled mess as always, with piles of magazines and picture-books (plus some tea cups I had glazed at school) strewn pell-mell across the floor. I was thinking about the tower and how long it had been since I'd leant out the window. I hadn't looked at it for ages. It didn't sing to my heart like it used to. I'd buried my hoop in the wardrobe as well. Sadness had taken me over, and I didn't know why.

This was the start of Year 9, my third year at Mount Carmel. Vivi, during my first two years, had been at Saint Mark's, a posh Sixth Form College in Stanley Park. But now she was gone, off on the train the day after my birthday, to study English Lit in Edinburgh. I missed her so much, but I knew I was going to miss her before she went. I knew there was more to my sadness than just that.

School had been a drag that day, as usual. Donna McGill had been a proper pain, sitting next to me all day, even though she wasn't my friend, and digging me in the ribs for no reason. 'She's trying to get me back for what I did to Martina last week,' I told myself. 'Well, if she tries it on again tomorrow, I'll send her flying like I sent Martina flying.'

Then there was Mandy Mitten, Mandy of the many problems: 'Julie, Mr. Sharp's always picking on me. Should I tell Mrs. Hunt?' 'Julie, Martina says I'm fat. Is it true?' And on and on and on …

I stood in my middle of my room and groaned out loud. Between Donna's elbows, Mandy's badgering and the teachers' boring lessons, I felt more dead than alive, a shadow of the joyful creature that just a few weeks before, in the gold and blue of August, had hurled the hoop up to the sun and caught it every time.

I peered through my fringe at the chimneys opposite. Telegraph wires in the alley quivered in the wind, carving geometrical shapes on the slate-grey sky. I thought about my Maths book and its baffling parade of rhomboids, hexagons, dodecahedrons and octagons – words and symbols that made no sense to me.

I bowed my head. Not in prayer, but sorrow. I knew now why I was sad. My life made no sense either. That joyous, playful Julie was dead. I'd buried her in the wardrobe, along with my hoop, a week before my birthday, the day Donna and Martina caught me playing in the Gardens. They teased and tormented me – Monday, Tuesday, Wednesday – till I lashed out with the back of my hand, bloodying Martina's knees on the playground's brittle shale. That was my childhood's first end. This was the second. I shut my eyes. I'd a crunching, grinding pain in the pit of my stomach. I felt like I was looking inside myself, or into the depths of the wardrobe where the hoop had its grave. Then something appeared. Inside me, I mean – a coal-black figure, tiny at first, surging from within, faster and faster, then charging at the speed of light. It rushed me like a mad thing, taking a shape and form that made me want to remember, there and then, every prayer Vivi had tried to teach me as a kid. I saw the outline of a skirt. I saw a loose bob, with a sweep from left to right. I screamed. Too late. The shadow had me. It swallowed me whole. I shuddered, flung back my head and keeled right over, scattering cups, books and magazines all over the place as I crashed to the floor.

When I woke, my heart was pounding so hard I thought it must have been Ma or Vivi hammering at the door. I couldn't have cared less if it was the Pope himself, the shitehawk. I was mad. Consumed. I wanted to smash, burn, destroy. I snatched a tea-cup, blue and white in Everton colours, and flung it at the wall above my bed. 'Fuck off,' I spat, as it shattered into pieces. I yanked open the door and shot across the landing, bounding down the stairs three at a time and storming out of the house just as I was, without a jacket and still in my uniform.

On and on I ran – wind streaming my hair, light sparkling my eyes – down the hill, past the Art School and through the Chinese Arch. When they found me, five hours later, I was standing by the water, clinging to the rail with shivering hands. Ripples bobbed and weaved with golden light but my eyes were fixed beyond, pinned to a point at the rim of the world where stars met water met sky. Dad's hand was on my shoulder. He looked out to sea with me, far to the West. Then the policewoman coughed and said it was time to go to the station. We turned around. The Liver Building was all lit up in white. It looked like a fairytale palace.

****

'Come on, Junior. Let's go for a walk.'

'But Dad, it's nearly tea. Ma'll be cross again.'

'Ah, be gone with you. She won't even know. We'll be five minutes, no more.'

We trotted down the steps and turned right. The tower stood solid and strong at the end of the street. A yellow car, parked by the concrete, box-like *Deutsche Kirche,* made me think of golden chariots in my picture-book Bible.

Soon we were stood beneath the tower, looking down on the city, watching the sunset singe and sting the whitestone façade of the Cunard Building. Dad was wearing a silver shirt and a black waistcoat. His long, fine fingers rolled a cigarette. He spoke softly, his blue eyes lodged on the city and the horizon.

'Tell me, my daughter – hand on heart – can these things be true your Headmistress tells me? You're out of control, she says – running amok – smashing tables and chairs, punching, kicking, even biting your classmates. You shout and swear at the counsellors. They've done all they can for you, she says. It's time to talk about your future, she says. So tell me, my daughter, can these things be true?'

I turned up my collar. Seagulls cawed. Hair whipped my face. 'They're true, Dad. I'm so sorry. I'm doing everything wrong, amn't I?'

I started to cry. He held me. He stroked my hair. Then he spun me around, pointed to the city and lit his ciggie. The smoke comforted me. 'You were looking out to sea, weren't you?' he asked. 'The night you ran wild in town.'

I nodded. Dad blew a smoke ring. I watched it fade into the flame-flecked sky, astonished by his words.

'Long ago, before I came to this city – before I came to Dublin even – when I belonged to the West still, I used to look out to sea myself. One night, around this time of year, I set sail for the horizon in your grandfather's little boat. Ah God, it was a rash enterprise, the sun going down and all, but the spell was on me, and what could I do? And I hadn't gone far before I was glad. Because there she was, the Sovereign Lady herself – Bridget of the Starry Eyes – goddess of music and stories, keeper of dreams and prophecies, walking on the waves and coming to greet me.'

'What did she do?'

'She told me a story.'

'What story?'

'Our story. The story I will tell to you in turn. The myths and legends of the West. I, my daughter, will anoint you a bard, the same way the goddess anointed me. Mrs. Hunt, you see, is a fine and feisty woman but she's short on imagination, like all the English. I told her I'd work some magic on you. It's a good time to start, I told her, the end of October. A man can walk through walls this time of year.'

He stubbed out his ciggie with his heel, gripped my shoulders, and turned to face me. His eyes were blue but wide and round like mine. 'There's nothing wrong with you, my daughter,' he resumed. 'You think you're too old to play with your hoop and your clothesbox, but you've nothing new in your soul to do what they did for you. You've nowhere to go with your vision and fire. What you need my girl are stories, stories to bring you back to the light, and, by all the gods at once, great Bridget gave me a wealth – Gaelic, Greek, Welsh – everything under the Shining One's gaze. Hearken then to my promise. Every sunset and dawn, from here on in, I'll walk you through this city and give you my continuations of the tales and yarns great Bridget set astir in my heart.'

He took my hand, ushering me along the forecourt and across Nelson Street. I expected him to make a start right there and then, but we walked down Rodney in silence instead. I ran my hand along the black railings. The houses looked posh and official, with gold plaques I couldn't make out in the twilight. The street lights came on. Their glare bounced up off the pavement and into my eyes. A knot of Far Eastern tourist types bustled by on the other side. Ahead and to the right, the bright spiky crown of the Catholic Cathedral – 'our Cathedral,' as Vivi called it – poked up like a blue and white beacon through the rooftops and aerials.

We came to the junction with Leece Street and stood at the crossing. The 75 bus shot past, down the hill and into the city.

'We've been miles longer than five minutes, Dad.'

'That's a grand looking house,' was all he said in reply. My eyes followed his finger. I saw a two-floor building across the road with five arched windows – three below, two above – with the bottom three dark but the top two bright with a warm amber light that showed me book-lined shelves, a few scattered chairs and a round wooden table.

A woman appeared, walked across the room from left to right and stood by the table. She wore a black robe with a red diagonal sash arrowing down from her right shoulder. Her hair was long and black, cascading down her back. She held a silver chalice. I gulped. She looked just like Vivi. She was talking to someone I couldn't see. Then she tilted back her head, drank from the chalice, walked past the table, and disappeared.

When she came back, a few seconds later, the chalice was gone. She stood in the window and looked straight ahead – face flushed, lips parted. She stretched out her arms and pulled the curtains tight, but not before I'd seen the golden crucifix on her neck. It *was* Vivi. But it couldn't be Vivi. Vivi was in Edinburgh. 'Dad,' I gasped, tugging at his sleeve, but the Red Man turned to green – beep beep beep – and Dad crossed the road. I scampered after him, and didn't get chance to look up again. The story had begun.

'In the beginning,' he said, 'in Tir-na-Moe – what you and me call the Otherworld, Julie – Bridget was singing. Angus and Midyir, Ogma and the Dagda and other princes of the sons and daughters of Dana hearkened to her song. And this is what she sang ...'

III

'Julie, Julie. There's sparkz flyin' round yer 'ead.' Mandy thrust out her arms, cheeks glowing pink in the frost, pigtails swishing her face. She ran from me and I watched her go, a shrinking speck in maroon and grey, bumbling through the bustling playground towards the security of the playing field.

I smiled, shrugged and swept back my hair, my hand a shield against the low morning sun. My shadow, stretching to the left, struck a defiant pose on the shale. Then another shadow – cocky and bold – joined itself to mine, thrusting out from my hip to the right. I looked up. The December sun glinted on Mrs. Hunt's glasses.

'It's lovely to see you so happy, Julie. You've a smile for us every day at the moment, it seems.'

The world went quiet around me. I scanned the playground. Everyone was watching. Damn and blast. I glanced at my shadow. It was merging into Mrs. Hunt's. I turned to face her again, noticing she had two blouse buttons undone (despite the cold) under her royal blue jacket. 'Your father's a remarkable man,' she said. 'He told me he'd work some magic on you, and by golly he has. Tell him he can have a job here any time.' She turned and strutted away, clapping her hands at the smokers, scattering them from their shelter by the Science Block wall.

I felt a new presence at my side. It was Billy Carter. 'What was all that about?' he asked.

'My Dad.'

'What about him?'

'I don't know.'

The bell went for the end of break.

'I don't want to talk about it,' I added, without knowing why.

Billy ran his hand through his choppy brown hair. We walked to the bag rack in silence.

Mrs. Hunt had been right though. I *was* happy. Very happy. Life made sense again. The world – thanks to Dad and his walks – was a better, richer, deeper, more exciting place than ever.

That joy must have shown in my face. Mandy hadn't been the first, after all, to look at me funny. There'd been the girl at the Sainsbury's meat counter, and Father Fox as well, both staring for ages – not at my eyes but my hair, or the sides of my hair – as if 'sparkz' really had been 'flyin' round me 'ead.'

Vivi was back for Christmas too. It was ace to be with her again. Everything was sound as a pound on Planet Julie.

****

'So,' said Dad, as we strode down the boulevard in the mist of a Boxing Day dawn. 'Rhiannon kept her distance from the king, riding at her own stately pace, while Pwyll, the Welsh King, whipped his horse, driving him faster and faster behind her but to no avail. The distance between woman and man, between his world and hers, remained as great as ever.'

He held my hand. Grass crunched beneath our feet. A splodge of yellow light, then a second, then a third, greeted the new day in the high steepling houses on either side. Street lights hung like little moons. A man in a white vest, in a top-floor window, lathered his face in a metal sink.

Then, like a mini Conwy Castle, the synagogue reared up at us out of the half-light, while over the road the Greek Church hovered and floated (unless my eyes deceived me) a metre or so off the ground. Behind its green domes my Guardian Angel, the Anglican tower, watched over the scene like an all-wise, all-seeing King.

I started to skip. I wasn't just hearing the story now, I was living it, a second Rhiannon, riding along in a dimension all of my own, where the kings (and queens) of this world could never catch me. I looked up, and my glance, for a second, took in everything around me: cathedral, church and synagogue. I was Queen of the City – nothing less – a brave and bold soldier girl, marching into Liverpool at the head of her very own army.

****

It was January, a wet and windy Friday evening. We walked down the steps and turned to the right. 'Dad,' I said, 'will you tell me that story again? The first one. When you showed me that house on the corner of Rodney and Leece.'

'Have you forgotten it so soon, my daughter?'

'I didn't hear it, Dad. I was too excited. I've got pictures in me head: a girl singing, and then a sword, then a spear, then a chalice, then a stone. But I don't know what happens or how they fit together.'

Rain pelted our heads. Wheels splashed. Headlights dazzled. Dad's hair blew white in the wind. His hand was on my shoulder again. But his eyes were moist; his voice sad. 'I can't tell you that one again, Junior. I can't tell you any of them again. They're given once and for all in the order the goddess gave me. The bard – that's you and me – has to add to the story he's given, tell it again his own way, then walk forward into the next tale. Legends and myths are live coals, my child, and the living chain of stories goes on and on. Bards don't ever go back. Only forward.'

I looked at him, and I loved him. There were so many things I wanted to tell him; so many things I needed to tell him: how much I adored him, how much I owed him, how much the stories were making me grow, how I didn't feel I needed my hoop anymore (love it though I did) and how he needn't worry or feel like he was failing his promise if he couldn't make it anytime because he had to go to work. But the words wouldn't come. I watched the raindrops trickle down his black leather jacket like little glow worms. 'Still,' he said, his eyes beginning ito brighten, 'it's a blessing you remember some of it at least. One day that story might come a-calling you, the same way Bridget came a-calling me.' We carried on walking. 'Let's have a look at Streatlam Tower,' he said, 'and that spiral staircase up the outside. I'll tell you the story of King Arthur and his raid on the Underworld.'

I lay awake a long time that night, gazing up at the crack in the ceiling. It was through a crack like that, said Dad, that Arthur and his crew had crept down to the Underworld to find and bring back the Sacred Cup.

I rolled over to the left. My schoolbooks lay higgledy-piggledy on the carpet with the magazines and cups. Starlight stole through the gap in the curtains, lighting up the tiger-lilies I'd doodled on the front of my French book.

Dad was working nights that week. I closed my eyes, thought of him and smiled. I pictured him perched in some eyrie of a Mess Room, high above Lime Street, swapping stories with his mates in their dark blue uniforms through the still, small hours.

I fell asleep. I dreamt. I was sitting in the eyrie with them. Knock knock knock on the door. Ma got up to answer. Ma? What was she doing there? The door opened. A cocky bold shadow thrust itself out across the floor. I looked up and screamed. Where Mrs. Hunt's eyes should have been were a pair of red spinning hoops. 'It's lovely to see you like this,' she said. I screamed again, lost my balance and fell, cartwheeling down in a figure of eight, black wind lashing my eyes. I looked for trains and tracks below, but neither came, just the blaze and bellow of a thousand roaring, leaping fires. Wild-looking women and men danced in the flames, brandishing burning rags – flags or fragments of clothes – twirling them around their horned and savage heads.

I screamed for the third time, then opened my eyes. I was flat on my back, back in my bed, looking up at the crack in the ceiling. My body felt like a sponge – hair glued to my forehead, t-shirt stuck to my skin – stickiness on my face, under my arms, down my legs...

Then the footsteps came. Behind the door. Soft but intent, like a big crafty cat. I sat up and snatched at the bedclothes till they folded around me like a pretend Roman toga. Knock knock knock. I stuffed my fist into my mouth. The door opened. A tall robed figure stood on the threshold, holding a lantern. I blinked, looked again, saw who it was and shook with relief as I took my fist from my mouth.

It wasn't a robe for a start. It was Vivi's green dressing gown. My sister held a phone in her hand as well, not a lantern. Its tiny screen cut a pink rectangle through the midnight gloom. Vivi's face glowed red, then gold in the peculiar light. Her hair was piled up high, twining round her head like a halo.

'Are you okay, Jules? I thought I heard you scream.'

'B-bad dream,' I stammered. 'G-gone now. Soz Vivi.'

The phone's light flashed off, then on again. I let the bedclothes fall around me. Vivi frowned. 'Dad's been telling you stories again, hasn't he?' I bit my bottom lip. Vivi shook her head. 'He shouldn't, Jules. It's dangerous.' She shut the door and came into the room, the pink rectangle stretching and expanding. 'Come on, Jules. I know you like the back of my hand. Imaginary worlds are real for you. You'll believe everything he tells you and muddle it up with daily life. You won't know whether you're coming or going.'

'S'not like that, Vivi. The stories make me better. Everyone says so.' I was going to add, 'even Mrs. Hunt,' but the memory of my dream chased the words away. I turned my head from my sister, defeated, and stared at the curtains.

'See what I mean,' said Vivi. 'It's upsetting you.' She sat down next to me on the bed. 'He told me that story too, you know, the one about the goddess and the boat, but I said I wanted to pray and he didn't bother any more. He likes telling stories, Julie. That's all. He likes to feel they matter, that they're real, that they make a difference.' She smiled. 'Moody teenage daughters give him the ideal chance.' I smiled too. I liked that. She rested her hand on my shoulder, just as Dad had done before. 'You shouldn't take him literally, Jules. Don't give yourself nightmares. I'll speak to him before I go and tell him to stop.'

The thought terrified me. I jumped up and flung my arms around her, burying my head in her long black hair. 'Oh, please don't, Vivi. Don't stop the stories. They're all I've got. My life'd be rubbish without them.'

The phone's light went out. Vivi ran her hand through my hair. 'Don't you think it's sad,' she said softly, 'that you say these stories are all you've got? They're supposed to make you better, yet you can't do without them. Sounds like a drug to me.'

I stamped my foot. 'No. Not a drug. The opposite.'

'Hush,' Vivi whispered. 'You'll wake them up.' She gave me a squeeze, gently disentangled herself from my grasp, then tightened her dressing gown belt. 'Why don't you try something different, Jules?' she said. 'Why not just sit in the Cathedral for an hour? When it's quiet and there's no-one there. One hour there's worth more than a thousand myths and legends, and Christ, if you ask him, will calm and settle your mind in a way these stories can't. Kings and heroes are no good. Not for you. They'll overheat your mind and make you mad.'

I bowed my head. Vivi's finely-moulded feet rattled me. I felt embarrassed by my stubby toes. I wanted to be on my own again.

'I'd better go,' said Vivi, as if reading my mind. 'Sure you wouldn't rather stay in my room tonight?'

'I'm okay now, Sis. Thanks anyway.'

She kissed me on the cheek and walked to the door, and something in the way she walked…

'Vivi.'

'Mmm.'

'Didn't I see you in that big house on the corner of Rodney and Leece a few weeks ago? On a Thursday evening.'

She spun on her heels, eyes flashing. 'Oh no,' I thought. 'I've made her cross.' But all she did was laugh, press a button and hold up her phone, forcing me to blink and squint in the pink light.

'See what I mean, Jules? You're all muddled up. You're a prisoner of fantasy.' She kissed me on the other cheek and ruffled my hair. 'Wait,' she said. She opened the door and left the room.

I flicked on the table-lamp and sat back down on the bed. Vivi came back, as I expected, with her King James Bible, her fave Bible since Sixth Form, even though she's such a big Catholic. Mr. Martin, her English teacher at St. Mark's, called it the 'Parthenon of English Literature', and I think she took her cue from him. I liked it too – the poetry, the music, the rich, rolling resonance of the language – miles better than the Bible they used at church and school. Vivi shut the door, stepped forward and read to me in a hushed, passionate, trembling voice:

'Now about that time, Herod the king stretched forth his hands to vex certain of the church. And he killed James the brother of John with the sword. And because he saw it pleased the Jews, he proceeded further to take Peter also. And when he had apprehended him, he put him in prison, and delivered him to four quarternions of soldiers to keep him, intending after Easter to bring him forth to the people.

'Peter was therefore kept in prison, but prayer was made without ceasing of the church unto God for him. And when Herod would have brought him forth, the same night Peter was sleeping between two soldiers, bound with two chains, and the keepers before the door kept the prison. And behold, the angel of the Lord came upon him, and a light shined in the prison, and he smote Peter on the side, and raised him up, saying, 'Arise up quickly.' And his chains fell off from his hands. And the angel said unto him. 'Gird thyself and bind on thy sandals.' And so he did. And he saith unto him, 'Cast thy garment about thee, and follow me.' And he went out and followed him and whist not that it was true what was done by the angel but thought he saw a vision.

'When they went past the first and the second ward, they came unto the iron gate that leads into the city, which opened to them of its own accord, and they went out and passed on through one street, and forthwith the angel departed from him.'

****

Alone again in the dark, I stood up, walked to the middle of the room and had a go at the exercise Miss DuVal had given us in Drama the week before. I breathed in for seven seconds, held for four, exhaled again for seven, held once more for four, then went to the window, whipped back the curtains, undid the catch and looked out. It was windy still, but the rain had stopped. A blue light flickered in the room opposite. Shadows shuffled behind curtains. I ignored them, leant out for the first time in ages and turned my head to the right. The tower – my Guardian Angel – was there again, super-imposed against the starry sky, big and strong like the giants in Dad's stories.

Cool air kissed my cheeks. I closed my eyes. Colours swished and swirled. Four images flashed by: a sword, a spear, a chalice, a stone, and then a fifth, a girl in a green headband and blue mantle blowing in the wind. She was sat on a rocky shore, singing. In her hands she held a harp. Tall, noble figures stood around her in a ring. The sky was blue and clear. Seagulls cawed. Waves splashed. I strained my ears to hear...

IV

'What did she sing?' asked Mr. Martin.

'I don't know, Sir. The more I listened, the less I heard. Everything faded and went. Then I was back in my room. It was cold, so I went to bed.'

We faced each other across the desk. Rain rapped against the windows – the wettest March since Thatcher's time, the teachers said. Mr. Martin rubbed his eyes. 'Old Sea Dog,' we called him in the St. Mark's Common Room, even though he came from Leeds, not the seaside, and wasn't actually all that old. His beard was only lightly flecked with grey, and his hair was almost as black as mine. But still, I knew what they meant. He wore a blue roll-neck jumper nearly every day. It suited his beard and sea-green eyes. Gina Calcanti, my best friend, swore she'd sneak up one day and scribble an anchor on the front. Then, she said, he'd look the 'proper spit' of Captain Haddock in the Tintin books.

'Is that why it haunts you?' he asked, pronouncing, as always, 'you' as 'yo'. 'Because you don't remember it?'

I drummed my fingers on the desk. 'It's because there's something missing, Sir. I've read the story since in books. Loads of times. But it's what's not in the books. That's what's missing. There was a bit in the story – when Dad told it – directly to do with me. That's what's missing, Sir. That's what's not in the books.'

Mr. Martin edged forward. 'Tell me it again,' he whispered. 'Slowly this time.'

'I've told you everything I remember, Sir. Bridget sings a song in heaven with the other gods and goddesses around her. But I never heard what she sung. In the books, after the song, they go down to the Earth with their treasures and create the world. But there was more than that when Dad told it, Sir. Miles more.'

'Concerning you?'

'Concerning me. But I wasn't listening. I only caught a bit of it. I saw something in a window and got distracted. When I asked him to tell it again, a coupla months later, he got all sad and said he couldn't, said he couldn't go back, only forward. Then I had that vision of Bridget at the window. I think about it all the time, but it hasn't come back and n-never will come back and, oh, what am I to do?'

I banged my fist down on the desk.

'Hush, Julie. Take it easy.'

I paid no heed. 'She gave Dad her stories, Sir. She made him a bard. That's what he said. So if I'd have been listening, if I'd have heard her song, then I'd b-be a bard t-t-too.' I scowled at the rain-spotted window. 'But I missed it. I got distracted. Then he died and everything stopped.' Rat-tat-tat went the rain. 'People don't look at me like they used to.'

I turned to him again, surprised to see his eyes so shiny and wet. Then I remembered what Gina had said: that his Ma had died, two and a half years ago, around the time we started at St. Mark's. Our eyes met. I looked away. But I heard what he said.

'I don't give a toss how people look at you. That's not my business. It's not yours either. Your business is to tell stories. Because you *are* a storyteller, Julie. Don't let me ever hear you say you're not.'

****

St. Mark's, as our Head, Sister Mary Margaret, loved to remind us, was founded in 1905 by Benedictine nuns. She's a Benedictine nun herself, of course, one of only three still there.

You'll find this religious vibe all over the campus, literally carved in stone above the door of every college building. The Science Wing, for instance, is called 'Olivet', the Business School 'Mount Tabor', and the Arts Cluster, where Mr. Martin and me sat facing each other in Room B6, 'Bethany'.

There's also a uniform, something which, by the time I reached nineteen (I'm twenty now), I found more than a bit irritating. But I have to confess it's a most stylish affair, and I miss it now I'm not there. There are worse things in life, I suppose, than swanning around in an electric blue blazer with your collars turned up and a winged golden lion facing down the world from your breast pocket.

This lion image, by the way, is the symbol of Saint Mark and it recurs repeatedly around the college. In B6, for example, there's an etching on the back wall. The lion's got his front right paw on top of an open book. The words on the page are the college motto: PAX TIBI MARCE, EVANGELISTA MEUS – Peace be with you, Mark my Evangelist.

I loved that. I couldn't get enough of it. Such class. Such quality. Such distinction.

Mr. Martin bent down behind his desk, reappearing with a pile of photocopied essays. 'Do me a favour please, Julie. Drop one of these off at each desk, will you.' I stood up and took the bundle. 'It *is* your group tomorrow at nine, isn't it?' he asked, looking at me like he was suddenly unsure, though I could tell he was only pretending and knew full well.

'Yes, Sir. It is.'

'*Trés bien.* 'Save us a job for tomorrow then. And seeing as you've been so good to come and see me after hours, you can take one with you and get yourself a head start.'

'Thank you, Sir.'

I weaved my way between the desks: twelve in all, set out in rows of three. The essay, I saw, was called *A Magic Carpet of Kings: Monarchy and Imagination in Macbeth*, by Ambrosius Carlisle. I hadn't heard of the writer, but the name 'Ambrosius' dinged a bell somewhere.

I popped the last essay on the last desk and stood at the back of the room with the lion behind me. B6, I should tell you, is one of the swishest rooms in the college. It's got four windows, two to the left and two to the right. The left-hand pair look out onto the quadrangle (I love the ivy clambering up the walls), while the two to the right show you the playing field. Not that you could see anything happening anyway, it was raining so much that particular day.

Cool, art-style prints in slim dark frames hung between the windows on either side of the room. The playing field side had an *Antigone* poster in French. A girl with flame-red hair stood with her back to the viewer, looking out at a copper-coloured helmet across a desert of yellow sand. The picture opposite was an ad for a stage adaptation of *Four Quartets*. It consisted of a set of interlocking rings – silver, gold, green and maroon – against a background of restrained, icy blue.

I turned my back on them both and studied my reflection in the playing field window. The raindrops on the glass made it look like I was crying.

'Thank you for coming,' I heard Mr. Martin say. 'I've been meaning to talk for a while. I wanted to find out what makes you tick; what makes you so imaginative. I don't think I realised your imaginative powers had such deep roots. I knew your father, of course, through parents' evenings mainly. I know he fed you a splendid diet of Gaelic, Greek and British myth. Your sister told me that. I'm not sure, however, that I quite appreciated the depths he sounded. I apologise, Julie.'

I sat on top of the desk closest the window. My legs swung back and forth – click click clack on its metallic legs. 'S'alright, Sir. I've always been like this. Since I've been a kid. My sister'll tell you that too.'

I sensed a sudden chirpiness in Mr. Martin's voice. 'How is Genevieve, may I ask? She went to Edinburgh, then London, didn't she, if memory serves?'

'She's doing a Masters in Christian Spirituality, Sir. At Heythrop College. She's been in France a lot too. 'Spent a year in a community there. Cooking for kids with Down's Syndrome.'

Mr. Martin clapped his hands. 'Excellent. Excellent. What does she hope to do when she's finished?'

'She wants to be a spiritual director, Sir. At retreat centres.'

A vacuum cleaner buzzed and hummed in Room B1 above. Outside, the rain had stopped. Goalposts stood white and wet at either end of the mud-spattered playing field. Orange netting bulged and billowed. A flag fluttered blue and gold on the half-way line.

The match! Oh God! The game against St. Oswald's at half-four I told Billy I'd watch.

Mr. Martin cleared his throat. 'Look, Julie,' he said. 'I know that Dr. Tenby has advised against it, and I respect his opinion, as you should too. I certainly side with him in that you should at least have made a deferred application. On the whole, however, I feel I need to give you credit for a brave decision. Between you and I, I think you've actually taken quite a shrewd option in not applying to university this year.'

My heels clicked rhythmically – clickety-clack. A patch of blue, over to the East, rolled around like a barrel of beer, shoving back the clouds and opening up the sky.

'Now, don't get me wrong,' he continued. 'Your intelligence is not in doubt. Quite the reverse. But you are – at this stage of your career, at least – far more creative than academic. There are precious few who could turn an essay on Macbeth at the witches' cauldron into an Arthurian meditation on past, present and future. That's remarkable by any standard.'

Hisssssss went the vacuum cleaner. Then *phhhhhutt*, as it collapsed into silence. Bluer and bluer grew the sky.

'So,' said Mr. Martin. 'I've got a suggestion to make.'

I turned my head. I missed the moment when the sun came out.

****

I was fifteen when Dad died. It happened suddenly, on a hot sunny day. That alone was enough to wreck my head. People aren't supposed to die on June afternoons, sun cracking the flags and what have you. Death belongs to winter, not summer, not the kind of day you unwrap a lolly-ice and turn the corner of your street, looking forward to some tennis on the telly and a long lingering sunset to stroll around and listen to stories in.

You don't expect to see an ambulance. Not outside your house. You notice your Ma in the middle of the road and the neighbours milling around. Your supercool sister's sat on the kerb with her head in her hands. No sign of your dad either. Where's Dad? 'Have you seen Dad, Vivi?'

Men in green come tumbling out of the gaff with a stretcher. There's something long and lumpy on it but you can't tell what because the sheet's pulled up. It's a grey sheet with maroon trimmings. Like your school socks.

Someone starts to howl and yelp. The greenies push on towards the ambulance but the someone's grabbing and clutching and clawing and thrashing. It's Ma. Oh Jesus. You turn and face the tower, but you can't look, you can't bear it, your Guardian Angel's let you down, and you know that it's over – *Finito* – you can't look at it again. So you sit on the kerb with your sister instead, offering what's left of your lolly. She doesn't hear you though. So you put your arm around her and finish it off yourself. It seems the only thing to do as you wait for all these silly people to piss off, and your dad to come walking round the corner to take you out, one more time, around the streets and squares of Liverpool 8.

****

A congenital heart defect. That was the verdict.

'Could have happened any time,' chirped the rosy-cheeked doctor.

'Let us thank God,' chipped in Father Fox, 'for granting Michael the time to spread so much of his *joie de vivre* among us.'

Time? What time? He was forty-seven.

I bombed. Disastrously. The next year, my GCSE year, turned into a near total write-off, saved only by spawny successes in English and History. When, at last, my head began to settle, I looked at my life and found myself in a right old stew. I couldn't see any way out.

'Think of a way forward, rather' said Sister Mary Margaret, when she invited me out of the blue to come and see her at St. Mark's. 'Forward and through. And listen, young Julie, don't go blaming yourself. Show some compassion to your poor bruised heart. The death of a parent, I know all too well, leaves an indelible mark. Like a brand. But at least I was thirty, then forty, when my mother, then my father, went to God. But you, my sweet thing, you were only fifteen. The loss of your father, if it wasn't for God's grace, would be impossible for you to live with. Fortunately, though, we know God's grace is alive in our world. All we have to do is ask for it.'

That's what she told me – that wise, white-haired, bright-eyed woman – and I shall forever be grateful to her, especially when my grades were so rubbish, for giving me the chance to make a new start.

I loved it at St. Mark's. Right from the off. The high-minded vibe sat well with me. Friends like Billy (who had also flunked his GCSEs) and Gina were loyal and true. I relished my studies in Drama, History and English Lit. But I had no desire to take things further and go on to Uni. I felt like I needed a break – the chance to read, think and write on my own for a bit, without the pressure of exams. I had already started to write my own stories, and I wanted to see where that took me. Besides, I'd found a nice job – working in the cafe at FACT – and I was meeting loads of arty types, both punters and staff, every weekend. I had no need of Uni.

Which is why it surprised me – the speed I turned my head at the word 'suggestion'. I thought I had the future sorted. Short-term stuff at least. Hadn't I?

Mr. Martin rolled up his sleeves and slapped down his big hairy hands on the desk's mottled wood. 'I can't understate how crucial it is that your time away from formal education is used creatively. It would be a crime, Julie, were you to blunt and lose your imaginative edge.'

The sun was irritating me. Getting in my eyes. I swivelled sideways on the desk to face him. 'What is it, Sir? What's your suggestion?'

'It's who, not what,' he growled, holding up Carlisle's essay and waving it at me. 'It's this man, Ambrosius Carlisle. I've known him since undergraduate days.'

'Who is he, Sir? What does he do?'

'Ambrosius and I are the same age. That's the first thing. He's from Newcastle; I'm from Leeds, as you know. We read English at York, completed our PGCEs together, and even taught at the same school for a while in Hull.'

Mr. Martin's eyes shifted across for a second to the *Four Quartets* poster. Now that the room was brighter, the rings stood out clearer and sharper. The maroon one looked like it was peeling away, like it had had enough of being stuck on the wall and wanted to sample the flesh and blood vibe of a cool, rainy March in L4.

'But he soon went his own way,' he continued. 'He was too independent, too free-spirited – eccentric, some might say – for conventional pedagogy. He was determined, I recall, to establish himself as an academic. But academia rejected him. Despite his clear genius. Having witnessed that travesty at close quarters, Julie, I have to say that's another reason why I think you've done well, for now anyway, in giving universities a wide berth.'

'What does he do now, Sir?'

'Well, we lost touch for a few years. I came here; he travelled in Europe – France and Russia, I believe. When we met again, seven years ago, he said he'd been writing, giving masterclasses, as he put it, in literature, performance and art. He lives in Manchester now. That's where I ran into him, at an English conference. His house is called Constantine's Chambers. It used to be a monastery. That's where he's built his artistic community.'

I jumped down from the desk. 'Is that what you want me to do, Sir? Join this community?'

Mr. Martin held up his hands. 'I want you to listen, Julie. Slow down and reflect.' He leant forward. 'Ambrosius views imagination as the highest faculty we have, a two-way street, he calls it, between the human and divine.' He smiled, folded his arms and sat back in his chair. 'Dr. Tenby, as we both know, would profoundly disagree. Historical events, Ambrosius argues, begin on the imaginative plane, then act themselves out in the material world. Our History School, as with most others, has it the other way round.'

He rested his hands behind his head and stretched out his arms at the elbows, like he'd won an argument. 'And I know you well enough by now, Julie, to guess which side you'd be on.' I nodded. I agreed. 'That is why,' he went on, 'with the best will in the world, Dr. Tenby's laudable attempts to steer you towards an academic career are doomed to fail. At least for now. And that is why I believe that a year in the company of Ambrosius Carlisle is exactly what your imaginative life requires. He sees the world through the same mythically-charged prism as you do. There's a synergy there, as they say over at Tabor. It's as plain as a pikestaff.'

He checked his watch, stood up, yawned, then crouched behind the desk, re-emerging with a sky blue raincoat in his right arm and a Marks and Spencer canvas bag in his left. 'Every year,' he said, 'in September, Ambrosius takes on a number of interns: actors, writers, painters, etcetera, for a year's collaborative study at Constantine's Chambers. You have to be between eighteen and twenty-six and you'll need to be prepared to live in-house with Carlisle and your colleagues. The project's funded by the EU, I'm told.'

'What'll he want me to do there, Sir? Write stories?'

Mr. Martin hauled the raincoat over his head. His salt and pepper hair jabbed up in spikes. 'I would have thought so, Julie. Wouldn't you? You do *want* to be a storyteller, don't you?'

'Yes, Sir. More than anything.'

'*Voila*! Maybe it would do you good then to know that last year the company rewrote Malory's version of the Grail mythos, setting it in Putin's Russia. There was a stage version of Yeats's Byzantium poems, a Bardic retelling of the Aeneid, and so on. Constantine's Chambers, in my opinion, Julie, has your name written all over it.'

I wrinkled my brow, trying my best to look thoughtful and blag myself some time. I think I'd already made up my mind to go, but there were a million and one reasons – all of them good, all of them noble – why I couldn't and shouldn't.

'Would you like me to speak with him?' Mr. Martin asked. 'I could even send him your *Macbeth* story. He'd like that.'

I swept back my fringe. 'I can't, Sir. I don't want to leave. Here, I mean. Liverpool. Not now. Maybe next year. Thanks though.'

Mr. Martin slung his bag over his shoulder and looked at his watch again. 'Don't be too sure of that, Julie. There might not be a next year. Things turn pretty quickly in this world. We both know that.' He brandished Carlisle's essay. 'It's all in Shakespeare,' he added, rolling it up like a scroll. '*Julius Caesar*, to be precise.' He looked me straight in the eye, paused, then recited: 'There is a tide in the affairs of men, which, taken at the flood, leads onto fortune.'

I closed my eyes, expecting a long speech. But no more was said. When I peered up, Mr. Martin was gone and the door, which had been open, was shut. Only brightness remained – shy, watery sunbeams playing games of light and shadow with the parquet floor. The doorknob shone like a little sun in its coat of polished bronze, and I remembered where I'd heard the name 'Ambrosius' before. He's Ambrosius Aurelianus, a character in *The Lantern Bearers*, by Rosemary Sutcliff, one of my very fave storybooks. He's a Romano-British fella who comes between Vortigern and Arthur and leads the Resistance against the Saxons. He wears a gold circlet around his head and that's what I've always remembered about him. I wondered, for a minute, if Ambrosius really was Mr. Carlisle's first name, or if he'd had it changed, maybe in honour of this great wartime leader?

Shouts and yells from outside tugged at my attention. The match! Oh rats. I looked out the window. The game had started. Gina, Bekki, and a couple of others were standing on the touch line watching. I saw Billy spray a pass out of play, then lose the ball to a St. Oswald's player, a barrel-chested, ginger-haired boy. Mr. Pattinson, the Sports Master shouted, shook his toupéed head and pointed. 'I'd better get out there,' I thought. 'He'll be wondering where I am. It'll be putting him off.'

I walked to the door. A yard from my goal, I stopped dead in my tracks. Someone was watching me. From behind. I turned around to face him (or her) down but no-one was there, just the lion on the wall. 'I've been imagining things again,' I thought. Then the lion – the cheeky piece – winked at me with his right eye. I looked again. No. He hadn't. Of course he hadn't. I'd been tricked by a dustcloud – that was all – pinned to the wall by a raking, golden, sunshine searchlight. 'Get a grip, Jules. You'll drive yourself crackers.'

I took another step and reached out with my hand. The bronze was warm to my touch.

V

'You stupid, stupid girl.'

'It's a tiny drop of water, Ma. Don't get a cob-on. It's nothing.'

'Nothing? You call that nothing? You've flooded the place. Everything's soaked.'

'It isn't. I haven't. You're just after an excuse. You can't wait to go to town on me.'

'Oh, so it's my fault, is it? My fault that such a clever girl with all her books and learning can't work a simple washing machine?'

'For Christ's sake, Ma. Stop having a go all the time.'

We glowered at each other, and the crude sun crashed through the curtainless windows. It was Friday afternoon, the day after my chat with Mr. Martin, though it felt a million and one years ago already.

I shook my head and lowered my gaze, watching the damp patch ooze and spread from square to square of torn, chipped linoleum. The washing machine juddered, convulsed, coughed three times and was still. Its round, port-hole window taunted me like the eye of the Cyclops. I could see my Pink Floyd t-shirt and Ma's red nightie wrapped around like soapy swaddling clothes.

A phlegm-fuelled cough rent and hacked the air. Ciggie smoke (Stuyvesant Red, *bleughhh*) hung heavy all around. Gavin, Ma's new friend, was sitting in Dad's chair in the living room, as usual. Maybe she saw the anger in my eyes. I don't know. She lunged at me anyway. I skipped back a metre, more from the smell of the whiskey than the threat she posed.

'You're your father's girl, you are.'

'What are you on about, Ma?'

'It's him you follow, not me. He charmed you like he charmed 'em all.'

'You're rambling, Ma. You're not making sense. You're drunk again.'

'How dare you say those words to me? Who do you think you are, you little hussy?'

It was desperate stuff. It really was. Ma looked so pitiful. So broken. Thin, raggedy remnants of hair flopped across her turquoise cardigan in lank, grey straggles. The unjust sun made the most of her criss-cross wrinkles. 'Get out,' she hissed. 'Walk into the sea. See if I care.'

'Stop it, Ma.'

'And find your sister while you're gone. Ask her why she left me, her supposed to be so holy 'n' all.'

'You're making things up, Ma. Stop it.'

She cocked her thumb at the living room door. The baccy smell seeped and poured into every nook and cranny of the house – harsh and acrid – nothing like the mellow rollie smells when Dad used to sit in that chair: *Cutter's Choice, Golden Virginia, Drum.*

'She's the cause of this, so she is. Saint Genevieve of Toxteth.'

'Oh, for Christ's sake, Ma. Wind your neck in, will you.'

I sprang forward, shimmied to the left and slipped past. I marched down the hall to the door and turned the cobwebbed handle. Raw light drowned us both.

'You stupid, stupid girl. You knew it. You knew it all the time. But you couldn't face it. You ran and hid in your books and stories.'

I stood on the top step, cold nipping my cheeks, too sad to even feel tempted to turn and give her some back. I focused on the terrace over the road instead. And that was the first strange thing that day. Those houses (that I'd seen almost every day of my life) looked totally, utterly unreal, like they'd been turned into a film-set or something, like all those balconies, pillars, plant pots and what have you might vanish into the back of some dodgy van at any moment.

'Your father conned you. He conned us all. Only Genevieve he couldn't con. She was different. She was my ...'

I didn't want to know. I slammed the door and strode down the steps. It was colder outside. I felt a splash, soft and squishy, just by my toe. A tiny tear glistened on the red and grey suede. I didn't even know I'd been crying.

I zipped up my blue Adidas trackie-top (the one with nice orange stripes down the arms), wiped my eyes and turned to the right. I felt like a proper teenager again, angsting about my rubbish life, comparing it to what Ambrosius Carlisle had written in his essay and how his sizzling use of words had made me buzz:

'Brighter than the fires of hell, fecund and fertile, more *puissant* by far than Macbeth's Satanic delusion, are these Shakespearian undercurrents, those deeper textures and rhythms at work in the play. Through their transformative offices, a salvific holy power enters the fray, with the King of England as the lynchpin, mid-point and bridge between the human realm and the Divine.'

I crossed Bedford Street and walked past the *Deutsche Kirche*, raising an eyebrow at my failed Guardian Angel. After it let Dad die, I swore I'd never look at it again, but it's hard to avoid – a whacking big tower at the end of your road.

It looked quite pretty, I had to admit, in the early-evening light. Brightness rippled its brownbrick surface, up and down like a shimmering curtain or veil. And that was the second strange thing. I looked around me, left to right and up and down, and the whole wide world now, plus everything in it, had turned into a film-set. The whole shebang – cars, houses, lamp-posts – everything I could see – stood on the point of collapse. Nothing was stable. Nothing was solid. The tower itself looked like it had been built out of Lego, the whole titanic mass poised to tumble, fall and splinter into a gazillion shards of wood and brick and glass.

'The end of this silly, stupid world,' I thought. 'Yay!'

And then came the third strange thing: a story welling up from within – first pictures, then words – clear, bright and sharp, like the sunrise in my childhood paradise – huge, colossal – five or six times its usual size...

****

... When the tower falls, I'll dodge the smoke and flying stones. I'll leg it through the gap, past the streets and houses, down to the sea with my hoop by my side. There's a ship with crisp white sails waiting there where sand and water meet. A rope-ladder quivers in the breeze between the shallows and the deck.

Once aboard, I look around and get my bearings. A vast ocean, streaked in sunset red and gold, extends about me. The sun's just like a tangerine. The sea-smell drives me wild. It reminds me of holidays in Southport and Llandudno, picking sea-shells on the beach with Vivi: silver, green and blue. My left hand shields my eyes from the sun. My right hand holds my hoop. I clamber down a wooden stairway next to the rainbow-coloured, diamond-patterned mast.

The ship seems so much bigger down below than up above. I walk for miles and miles down corridors lined with lush, milky-silver carpets. Lamps like little planets swing from panelled walls. I walk past a solemn door of sturdy oak. The ship starts to move, bobbing up and down as I glance to my left. 'Surely,' I say to myself, 'only a wizard, a King or a High Priest, like the ones in Dad's stories, could live and work behind such a mysterious door.'

I see a painting in a gilt-edged frame, just past the door, showing a boy in a white tunic with a fire-red angel on the front, swooping down from heaven, shining sword in hand. A scaly dragon blows back smoke at him from below.

There's another gold-framed piccie by the next door. A winged horse, like Pegasus in the Greek story, flies across the mountains through a star-packed sky. Riding on his back is a girl with flaxen hair, green t-shirt, bare feet and blue three-quarter length jeans. I scrutinise her face for ages, thinking I know her from somewhere, but I don't, and I carry on, up and down winding, wooden staircases, in and out of handsome chambers illustrated with beauteous tapestries of interlocking, interweaving symbols of gold and burnished red. I sit in spacious throne-rooms like a Queen. I crawl like a scullery maid through boxy cubby-holes, the only sounds my trainees squeaking on the floor and the splish splash splash of waves outside. The ship moves swiftly now, but I'm losing the sense of time and struggling to remember the days and years, if ever there were any, when I wasn't in this place. It feels like I've always been here and always will be. Before I was born and after I die

I reach a dead end. The wooden walls narrow to a point. There's a door to my left, just like the others, with a picture beside it as well, a smudged-crayon drawing of a ballerina – tall, poised, primed to take off into flight – hair bound up in a round brown bun – arms, chest and head arching forward, up and out to the circular window above and the sunlight rushing through.

I've butterflies in my stomach now, snakes almost, and I don't know why. It feels like the room's pulling me in. There's a bronze handle, like a big ring, half way up the door to the right. I turn it this way, then that, then the door clicks open and I'm standing on the threshold looking in. The first thing I see is the round port-hole window to the right – sky above, sea below and the line of the horizon dividing the two. I enter the room. The walls and floor are made of stone. I look around, then gasp and catch my breath. A figure's standing in an archway with her back to me, two metres off at the end of the room. I can tell it's a 'her' because I know who it is. I've seen her like this before, you see. She's in a white robe this time, with a purple diagonal sash. Dark, wavy hair flows down her back in lustrous streams. There's a table in front of her, hung with cloth of gold that flutters in a breeze I can't sense or feel at all.

I walk forward, and Vivi turns to face me. In her hands she holds a silver chalice, so bright I stumble back and fall. I scramble about on the floor, groping blindly for my hoop. But it isn't there. What've I done with it? Where've I left it?

'Vivi, Vivi, I've lost my hoop.'

I crawl on the ground like a baby. Silver light burns grey stone white. I sweat. I shake. Then he comes – a coal-black silhouette – tiny at first, hurtling up from the deep places – faster and faster – charging at the speed of light – rushing like a mad thing. I scream. Or think I do. But it's a different voice I hear. A voice from ages past. The voice of sea-shells on the beach:

'You haven't lost it, Jules. You'll never lose it. It's where it's always been. Where it always will be. The altar of your heart.'

I pick myself up and stand before my sister. The shadow, thank the gods, has gone, banished forever by Vivi's holy power.

I can see again. Silver rays shoot around the room like spokes on a wheel, but it isn't a problem now. I can look directly at the chalice and straight into my sister's wide, round, gemlike eyes. She holds the chalice out.

'Come and drink.'

I kneel down, take a sip and hand it back to her, not because it's horrible – not at all – but because a sip is all I need. It's the strongest drink I've ever tasted. By a million, million miles. Stronger than vodka, puccine, anything.

Peace and stillness descend upon me. Breathing slows and deepens. Eyes close, sparks I see, then Dad's face right before me, hair white and bright, eyes sapphire blue. 'Thank you, Dad,' I try to say, 'I won't forget you, I'll always be with you.' But no matter how hard I try, no matter how loud I shout, the words don't come. Dad's face fades. Slips back to black. 'Dad, come back. Don't go,' but he's gone, and now it's Ma's worn-out, weary features accusing me. 'I'm sorry, Ma. I'm so, so sorry,' is all I can say, and I know it's not enough, but her face disappears into dark in its turn, as calm and quiet surround me again, and it's good, very good, all good. I know, deep down, between you and me, that everything's okay and the story of my life is panning out exactly as it's written in the stars. But that doesn't mean I'm always happy, or that I don't feel the pain of things. Christ no. No way. The wine, or light, or whatever it is, makes me feel it more than ever. Dad''ll never take me out again – never never never. All I've got now are rows and wretched shouting matches.

Then comes the third face – bearded, noble, regal – like the wizards, kings and priests that turned me on in his stories. But I'm crying now again, the vision goes all misty, the kingly face vanishes.

I feel sick. Bleughhh. My body jerks and heaves on the slabs. The ship dives down, then soars back up.

'Don't fight the tears,' says Vivi. 'They'll wash you whiter than the snow. They'll cleanse you from the trials behind you and strengthen you for those to come.'

She holds the chalice out again. Our fingers brush together.

'Drink, my sister.'

I take a sip, a big sip, almost a gulp, and the world turns white around me ...

****

I opened my eyes, blinked, looked to my left, looked to my right, felt the cold kiss my cheeks and remembered where I was. Everything seemed straight and normal again: the tower strong and monumental, the houses, cars and lamp-posts friendly and familiar. The atmosphere had lost its weird intensity. I shivered and wrapped my arms around my shoulders, wishing I could zip my trackie-top up further still.

A man came walking towards me down the street. He smiled and nodded. I nodded back. He had on brown, square-toed shoes; faded jeans; a salmon-pink shirt; and a crumpled, blue serge suit jacket. His face was lined and craggy, and his hair was like a lion's mane – mainly grey but streaked with random patches of both black and white. It flowed onto and over his collar. I had no idea how old he was. But I liked him straightaway. He was noble. Kinglike. 'Now, there's a face,' I told myself, 'that I could hang a proper story on one day.' I remembered to smile, but he had already gone past, his three-tone mane receding from my sight as he cracked on towards the Gardens.

Seagulls called from high above, like they were cawing out my name – *Joooleee, Joooleee*. I watched them wheeling round the tower's topmost turrets. Wind flicked my fringe. I walked to the end of the street, then turned right onto Hope Street, heading for the Cathedral. I knew there and then what my next job, the following day, needed to be.

VI

'We're not going in, are we?' said Billy.

I shook my head. 'Nah, we'll just walk around the top for a bit. It'll be quiet up there.'

I craned my neck. The Cathedral – that glass and concrete pyramidic sky rocket – dwarfed us in grey and white. The *Piazza* café to our right was all a-bustle, as usual, with its Saturday afternoon mix of tourists, old-folks and kids. A man with white bushy hair, like a prophet out of the Bible, sat smoking at a table outside.

Fifty-seven exceedingly wide steps run up from the bottom, where Billy and I were standing, to the great doors at the top. I'd climbed them often, over the years, having taken Vivi's advice to heart. She'd said I should sit inside for an hour, but, to be honest, I preferred it outside, walking around the top.

Don't get me wrong though. The inside's lovely – circle-shaped, with long, curvy benches fanning out from the High Altar in the middle. Everywhere's cool and dark, but quivering with light as well. Slim, blue, vertical stained-glass strips line the circle, as blue as the Sea of Galilee in my picture-book Bible. If you sit there long enough, you'll see flashes of red, like salamanders or Hebrew letters, spring to life on the blue, while high on the walls, the tapestries flow and stream around: Our Lady of Liverpool, Christ holding open the Gospel, flakes of fire falling upon the Apostles' heads, and so many more.

Tilt up your head to the top of the cone, the bit that looks like a crown from the outside. Watch all the colours rotate and revolve in the light: red with white tints to the South, yellow and green to the East, blue and purple to the West, and a mixture of all (except red) to the North.

It's a beautiful, stunning sight, yet it doesn't deep down turn me on. Not fully. It doesn't get the juices going, not like being outside, high above the city. Up there's like Gorsedd Arberth – the magic mountain – where, Dad said, King Pwyll sat one morning, watching from a throne of cobalt blue, his spearmen around him in a ring, waiting for Rhiannon to come riding out of the mist again on her milk-white mare.

****

Up the steps we went. I followed the curve of the building around to the right. Billy walked beside me to the left. Huge white buttresses, thicker than tree-trunks, jutted out and down to the ground. I swerved towards the low wall overlooking the Uni, stopped and took the plunge.

'I've changed my mind, Billy. I'm going to Manchester. If they'll have me, that is.'

He grabbed my left arm, just below the elbow. 'You're joking me?' he said. I ducked my head and avoided his eyes, feeling the pain in his confused, disappointed grip.

It was a bad do. All my fault. I'd led him on for ages, and now, no matter how much I wriggled and squirmed, the last thing I could see was a decent way out.

'You could cut steel on Billy Carter's cheekbones,' Gina, from time to time, liked to whisper in my ear. But the phrase, along with the wink and the nudge that came with it, cut no ice whatsoever. I had never, you see, had any intention of 'going out' with Billy. He was a friend – a special friend – like Gina herself. Nothing more.

I admit though, that I'd done very little, over the years, to make that clear. Let's be honest. I enjoyed the attention. And look, there's a lot of nice things about Billy. But to me, you see, he's just a boy. A lovely boy. One of the best. But still, a boy. And that's the problem. I'm not into boys. Boys are so immature. Gadgets, games and gormless expressions. That sums them up for me.

When I think of men on the other hand, men like Dad or Mr. Martin, or even Dr. Tenby, who's a very old man indeed, well that's a different story. Not that I 'fancy' any of them or anything like that. But there's character there – in their faces – depth and intelligence. That's what I'm after. That's what it's about. Not being 'pretty' or 'nice'. That's kids stuff. Cuts no ice.

There was no way I could get any of this across to him though. Especially not now. My reply, when it came, was pissweak and feeble. 'Look Billy. It's been the hardest decision I've ever had to make. I've thought about it for days and days.'

He tightened his grip and the tide of my mind started to turn. He was getting on my wick now, bossing me about like I was his own private property. 'Sea Dog spoke to you on Thursday,' he shouted. 'That's not days and days. You can't have thought about it. Not properly.'

I wriggled my arm free, then shoved him in the chest. Billy stumbled back, his mouth a little 'o' of shock. I wagged my finger and gave it him both barrels. 'Listen little boy, if you were in my shoes, if your Ma was a pisspot, living with some stinking waste-of-space fella, you'd get out too. Your feet wouldn't touch the ground you'd be out so quick.'

Billy slipped his hands inside his pockets, crossing one mauve Fred Perry sneaker over the other. I sensed a sudden, devious hope in him. My heart sank. I knew what he'd say. It was all so predictable. 'Why don't you just move out then?' he said. 'What about Bella? She's looking for a place of her own. You could share.'

I groaned and walked away. 'That's boys all over,' I thought. 'It's all so easy for them –do this, do that, put this piece here, that piece there – so practical, so rational, yet miles and miles from anything that truly matters.'

I crossed a sea of paving stones at the back of the Cathedral and stood by the far wall. Billy followed. The University tower faced me across Brownlow Hill. The clock on the top's got black Roman numerals, golden hands and a soft green background. It shines like silver on a sunny day. But this day was grey. Five to three said the clock. 'Look, Billy,' I said. 'It isn't just Ma. It's this place too. Liverpool. It feels small now. I don't know why. It just does. I wish it didn't.'

'Small?' he replied. 'You call this small?' I kept looking at the clock. I knew what he was doing – pointing down to the city – Albert Dock, Liver Building, blah, blah, blah.

I was right. 'There's nothing like this in Manchester,' he said. 'It's a shithole. A load of glass and steel. Don't go, Jules. They're hard-faced fuckers, the Mancs. They'll laugh at your stories and rip you to shreds.'

I'd had enough. I lost it with him, good and proper: 'No-one rips me to shreds, Billy Carter. Do you hear? No-one laughs at my stories either. I've been through too much for that. Now look, I'm not going there to piss you or anyone else off. I'm going 'cos of Mr. Martin. He knows me. Knows my mind. Knows what I'm capable of. There's nothing here for me anymore: not FACT, not Gina, no-one, nothing, not even...'

I was going to say 'Uni', but Billy nipped in first. 'Me,' he said, with sad, puppy dog eyes. The clock struck three. I felt like a bitch.

A 790 bus – a sickly blend of green and blue – waited for passengers below. No-one got on. The doors shut. The bus didn't move. I stuffed my hands in my pockets and bustled past him, carrying on left around the Cathedral, unable once again to look him in the eye.

Wind whipped up, whistling my hair. I looked left. Across the concrete sea, on the back of the Cathedral, was a big brown cross, with a barestone altar beneath. I hadn't seen it before, or if I had, I hadn't noticed it. I wondered why. Its bareness and simplicity impressed me.

I followed the building's curve, under the buttresses, then looked right, catching a glimpse of low-roofed houses and gorse-flecked gardens. Then the Liverpool Science Park, with its off-white plaster and massive glass windows, cut out the view. Through a gap, a few metres along, the Liver Building appeared, as I knew it would. It's bottle-green, mosque-like domes and painted birds looked distinctive and distinguished in the steel-grey sky. But by then I'd come nearly all the way round, back to the fifty-seven steps. The Anglican – stately and composed – sat like a king at the bottom of Hope Street, the tower a pin-point silhouette. 'You could cut more than steel on that,' I mused, as I watched a little ball of light roll and swell behind the heaving banks of cloud.

I didn't hear and didn't sense Billy rush me from behind, but in a second he had both my arms pinned behind my back. 'Ow! Gerroff.' He twisted me around and shook me like a doll. I kicked and struggled and pushed and shoved.

'Christ, Julie,' he roared. 'What is it with you? You can't live in this stupid dream world forever.'

I booted him in the shin with the back of my foot. He let go, hopped back, and squealed like a schoolboy.

'Why can't you get it into your thick male head? I'm not the one living in a dream world. My world's real – my imagination and the stories in it. It's your world that's stupid. The so-called real world. That's what I'm leaving behind. And you know what, Billy? I can't fuckin' wait.'

'Do one then. See if I care. You'll soon come crawling back. Fairy tales don't pay the bills.'

'The bills are paid for, divvy.'

I clocked, out of the corner of my eye, of a knot of people watching by the Cathedral doors. A fat-faced, middle-aged fella in a beige cashmere jumper smacked his hands against his thighs, mouth wide open in merriment.

'If your world *was* true,' countered Billy, 'you'd see what everyone else can see.'

'Oh yeah? What's that then?'

'Sea Dog's after you. It's obvious. He fancied your sister too. Everyone knows that.'

'Do they? Well, no-one's told me. That's a disgusting thing to say. How dare you say such words to me? That's not the Billy Carter I know.'

Billy held his arms out wide, as if appealing for forgiveness. 'It *is*,' he pleaded. 'It's the Billy who cares for you. The only Billy there is.' His bottom lip trembled. Despite everything, I was touched. 'You're different, Jules. Different to all the others. You're off your head, but that's alright. That's what makes you special. That's what makes you you.'

I put on a sulky face. 'I didn't ask you to care, did I?'

'You never ask for anything, Jules. That's your problem. You're too proud. Like you said one time, you think you can walk through walls.'

'Did I? When?'

Billy ignored my question. 'You were glad enough of me when Donna and Martina were at you, weren't you? And when your dad passed away.'

The group of observers disappeared down the steps. 'Nothing to see here,' I felt like shouting.

'You're right, Billy. I'm sorry. I'd have been lost without you and Gina. I know that.'

He held my hands in his. 'Then stay,' he said. It was hard not to be swayed, if not by his words, then by his soft brown eyes, 'If you go, then everything'll change. This Constantine's Chambers place – it sounds like a cult to me. Honest, it does. It'll change you, Jules. It'll change me. We'll lose what we've got. We'll lose what's special.'

I wanted to tell him not to worry, that it wouldn't be a problem, that everything'd be okay, that Manchester wasn't far, that I'd come back at weekends and we'd still be close. But that wasn't what I said. Not at all. I was appalled by what I said. 'There's nothing special,' I said. 'Never was, never will be. We're friends. That's it. Nothing more. And I *am* going to apply for Constantine's Chambers. I'm a storyteller. A bard. I need action and adventure. Nothing's going to stop me.'

This time I didn't need to struggle. Billy had already let go. But the madness was back. He whirled his arms around like a drunken Samurai. 'So that's what it's all about,' he blazed. 'Not exciting enough, am I? Not a writer. Not an intellectual. You're letting some arty dickhead give you one, aren't you? Admit it. Someone who lives in Manchester innit? That's what it's all about. Admit it. Admit it.'

I stamped my feet and jumped up and down. My fringe lost its shape and collapsed over my eyes in a black soggy mess. 'Jesus, Billy, no. That's not it at all. No way.'

Billy wound back his arm. I braced myself, but no blow came, just a gust of wind and the sound of his sneakers smacking on the steps as he fled. He sped across the forecourt, then crossed Mount Pleasant blind. A blue and white stripey 'smart' car skidded and beeped. The driver – a girl with curlers in her orange hair – slammed her fist on the dashboard and stormed out onto the road, but Billy was gone, running on, past the Everyman, past the Philharmonic pub, ducking left onto Hardman Street and vanishing from sight.

'Fuck fuck fuck.' I swept the hair from my eyes and slapped my cheeks again and again until I felt the tears sting. A posh-looking woman in a leopard-print coat came out of the Cathedral, stared at me for a second, then scuttled back inside.

I was furious with myself. I couldn't begin to fathom what I'd done – why I'd been so savage, hard and cold. 'Christ almighty, I'm turning into a monster.'

I sat on the top step. 'Vivi was right. The stories have driven me mad. I used to fancy myself as a second Rhiannon. More like the Minotaur now.' I looked down at the forecourt. The Biblical prophet had gone. 'It's the Dolourous Blow. That's what it is. And now I'm cursed, like Geraldine, bound in fetters till the chosen boy or girl comes to break her chains.'

I buried my head in my hands. Dad's voice came to comfort me, breaking his own rule, telling me Geraldine's story for the second (and last) time...

****

'Geraldine bolted through the great stone hall, the Grail King's footsteps clattering behind her. She couldn't fathom what she had done wrong and why he was chasing her. Tears ran from her eyes as she ran, ran and ran – long brown hair lashing around her face – up spiral stairways, down carpeted corridors, through high, vaulting chambers, in and out of candle-lit chapels, gilded with gilt-edged chalices and crucifixes. All the time, though she was running faster than she could ever remember, she made no distance on the King at all, though he was so much older and heavier than she. If anything, he appeared to be gaining.

'She came at last to a winding staircase, stretching up and up so high she thought it might never end. She heard the King's sword clashing against the narrow walls. Her spirit shook, but still she ran – faster and faster, higher and higher – blood boiling in her head. She reached the top and stopped before a wooden door without a handle. She pushed, and the door flew open, flinging her forward

onto her hands and knees in a corridor of grey, silent stone. She crawled away to her left, shattered and disorientated, forgetting to shut the door behind her.

'She stood up, after a while, and leant against the wall for support. To her left stood a door, like the one she had opened before, but with a handle this time – a big iron ring – half-way up and a little to the right.

'The sword rang louder in her ears. Geraldine marched forward, turned the handle and opened the door. At first she saw nothing, the room was so bright. She protected her eyes with her hand. The King's sword clashed again from behind. Then came a voice from the heart of the light. 'Stop. Come no closer. You are not yet ready.' Geraldine looked around, but couldn't see anyone, it was still so bright. She crossed the threshold and closed the door. She found neither lock nor handle on the inside. She hoped that the King, in his rage, would run straight past.

'Slowly, her eyes became accustomed to the light. Under a stone arch, fifteen feet ahead, was an altar draped in cloth of gold. Two candles flickered and quivered, one to the left and one to the right. Geraldine, for the first time in a long time, felt happy and still inside. But not for long. She remembered the King, and as soon as she did, there he was, hammering on the door and appearing at the entrance. The silver band in his jet black hair glittered in the reflected light, but the venom and hatred had departed from his face. He gazed at the altar like a man in a trance, and it was that, my daughter, more than anything else, that made Geraldine mad. 'How dare you follow me here?' she screamed at him. 'How dare you steal my special, holy moment? It's mine. Not yours. Mine.'

'She turned from him. Her vision grew yet clearer. She beheld a rough-hewn stone, like a boulder, on the floor, at the foot of the altar. Next to it lay a dazzling, sharp-looking sword, with a purple and blue jewelled hilt, while behind the altar, fastened to the wall, pointing up, was a golden spear with a blood-red tip.

'Geraldine couldn't take her eyes from the spear. She knew what she wanted it for. She knew it was wrong, but that didn't stop her. She ran around the altar and unfastened the spear. 'Touch not,' commanded the voice, but Geraldine was too filled with fury to hear or care. She hurled herself at the King, stabbing him in the thigh, over and over again, revelling in his screams and the agony wracking his face. His sword fell to the floor. The echo was a bell, a summons in her head. The world grew cloudy and dim, then black as pitch. A great wind blew, flinging Geraldine from floor to wall and back again, until her mind, spirit, soul and body cried out as one in pain.

'Down she fell – down, down and down again – until she smelt, then saw, the fires of Hell licking at her feet. Wild-looking men and women raged and bellowed in the flames, whirling burning rags around their horned and savage heads. Geraldine's roar of horror and woe was lost in the barbaric din as they bound her tight in adamantine chains.

'And that, my daughter, concludes for now, the story of the Dolourous Blow that laid ten kingdoms waste. Prophets, so they say, *have claimed that a girl or boy will come at the end of the age, whose high destiny it is to descend into Hades, break Geraldine's chains and restore Britain, Ireland, Europe, and the whole wide world to the eternal, ancient light.'*

****

Heat and light kissed the top of my head. I took my hands from my face, squinted, and looked up. The wall of cloud was broken. Sunlight streaked across my skirt, leggings and pumps. I took a pack of *Cutter's Choice* from my pocket, then my Rizlas, rolled a ciggie and had a think. That was the last story Dad had told me, you see, strolling through Sefton park on a bluehaze Thursday in June, the stream tinkling away, plink plonk plank, to our left as we walked. Geraldine was Ma's name too. I'd meant to ask him why he'd used that name, but I started going on about something else I can't remember now. Six days later it was too late.

I got my lighter out. A red rubber ball bounced past me, thump thump thump down the steps to my right. A little girl in white with a thatch of bright blonde hair ran after it. 'Come back ball,' she called. 'Don't run away.'

'Gemima,' barked a woman from behind my head. 'Come back 'ere this minnitt.'

Gemima raced down the steps like a cheetah-cub. But the ball was faster. It bounced along the bottom, then hopped and rolled across the forecourt towards the tables. A woman with tinted yellow hair, high heels and the biggest, silliest earrings I'd ever seen was standing above me to my left. 'Wait till you have kids, hun,' she blustered. 'You won't get time to sit 'ere thinking of nothin' then.'

Gemima pounced on the ball and held it up like a trophy. 'Gemima,' yelled her mother, careering down the steps in a pair of pink, way-too-high heels.

She got there though, and once mother, ball and child were happy and reunited, I got up and started heading down the steps myself, reflecting on the day's events.

'What a mess' was my verdict. 'I'll tell you this as well. Whoever that boy or girl is who's supposed to do all those things, I'll bet you any money it won't be me.'

I turned right at the bottom, down the hill and on into town.

I sat on the steps of St. George's Hall, counting the columns around me: seven to my right, four to my left. Liverpool – a magic urban carpet – unfurled itself below me, basking like a moggy in the afternoon sun. Buses – some yellow, some bluey green – zipped around the streets. Engines whirred, rattled, squeaked and squealed. Punters shuttled in and out of Lime Street. The sun was out. The city looked a picture. Renshaw Street, to my right, reached up and out to the bombed-out church and its sensitive, slim-line tower. The Anglican hulked like a brooding hen above, like it was jealous 'cos it had caught me looking at another tower.

Well, it could 'do one,' as Billy had said. My eyes were fixed the other way now, straight ahead at the curving roof of Lime Street Station. Through sun-splashed glass partitions, I glimpsed the fuzzy shapes of trains, the tracks uneven markings and the hazy outlines of limestone walls and tunnels beyond.

A 790 bus wheeled out and around of Paradise Street to the right. The city was gorgeous – heartbreakingly so – beautiful, sad and glorious all at the same time. There isn't a better city on earth. Or in Heaven, I'm sure.

Yet I was leaving – I knew it, I felt it. Yet I was glad – excited and energised.

I lit my ciggie and blew out a smoke ring. It seemed the only thing to do.

VII

So there I was, six months later, sat on the Manc train as it shuttled through the tunnels. October 1st sunshine flickered and flashed on moist, mossy walls from narrow slits of bridges overhead. I pressed my face to the glass, sports bag and suitcase tucked up on the luggage rack above. The fella to my right – a tall bloke with steel-grey hair – scanned the letters page of the *Echo* and paid me no attention.

The world, between bridges, turned shadowy and dim. My reflection pressed back, pale and luminous in the darkened window. I readjusted the red bandana so it sat a little looser. I was chuffed to have it on my head again. It was a miracle. An omen. A blessing. Vivi, of course, used to say it made me look like a pirate, but I'd gone for a different look that day for some reason, rolling it into a headscarf and knotting it at my forehead in vintage washerwoman style.

I reached into my pocket (I was wearing a white Tacchini tennis top, by the way, with blue jeans and red and white pumps) and pulled out Vivi's letter for the millionth time. Even though she didn't like what I was doing, and had told me so again and again, I still thought it brill of her to actually sit herself down and write me a letter. To be honest, I just liked looking at the words on the page. A certain refinement – the flowing italics, maybe – set a spark aglow in me:

My Dearest Julie,

It has been such a lovely summer. I have enjoyed our talks so much. I only wish, at the end of it all, I could concur with your conclusion regarding Constantine's Chambers.

I wish you every blessing. You know I do. But I would counsel you one last time not to depart for Manchester. You know my opinion. Your interests lie, as far as I can see, in signing a longer contract at FACT and preparing yourself for University next year.

From what you tell me, and from what I have ascertained on the web (and other places), there is a cult-like quality to Constantine's Chambers and a definite cult of personality surrounding Ambrosius Carlisle. I hesitate to set myself against Mr. Martin, but it can't be denied that he is, in his own way, as over-imaginative as both yourself and Dad, He is also, of course, a close friend of Ambrosius Carlisle, and therefore all too keen, I imagine, to do him favours and send him 'students'. You should, if I may say so, have attended to Dr. Tenby's words, and I urge you again to reflect on the very sound advice he gave you.

I appreciate that living at home is not easy, and I acknowledge that I am far away and unable to share the load. This is something I often reflect on. Am I away too much? Do I come back often enough? Will Mum be okay if you leave as well?

I wish, dear Julie, I really do, that I could spend more time in Liverpool. There is nothing I would like more. But this is my calling and my vocation, and I need, unfortunately, to be here. All I can do is promise to come back every couple of weekends. That means we'll see each other lots and lots if you stay.

I do hope you stay, Julie. But I recognise and understand the thirst for adventure that drives you. In which case, all I can say is good luck and keep in touch. Don't be a stranger. Remember I'm always here for you. Day or night.

I'm going to tell you a secret now, Jules. Remember when we went through the clothesbox a couple of years ago? Well, I saw the red bandana before you did, and just couldn't bear to let it go. It reminded me so much of the happy times we shared as kids. So, I popped it in my pocket and promised myself I'd surprise you with it one day.

Well, that day's come, and here it is, a token of the bond between us. I hope you have fun with it. You always did!

My dearest Julie, I wish you every blessing for your adventure. At this time of Michaelmas, may St. Michael and all God's holy angels watch over, guide and protect you.

All my love.

Yesterday, today, tomorrow, always,

V x

I folded up the letter and returned it to my pocket. The train, tooting triumphantly, burst free from the tunnel, bolting into sunlight as it rampaged through a deserted Edge Hill station. Its brownbrick/yellowpaint combo was past me in a flash.

I reflected again on Vivi's advice. What she'd said, in many respects, was spot on. I could, if I wanted, get off at Wavertree, go back to FACT, apply to Uni for the year after (I got three 'A stars' amazingly), and spend the next twelve months reading, writing, chilling and putting up with things as best I could at home.

Which was exactly what Dr. Tenby had suggested when he phoned me the day after the results and asked me to come and see him. Let me tell you a bit about Dr. Tenby. His first name's Ronald (Mr. Martin's 'David', by the way) and he's got white, shaggy hair sprouting all over his head. He's the only teacher at St. Mark's to have an office of his or her own. Why, I don't know. I think he's from London originally, because when he says 'Now then', it comes out as '*Nah* then', but I've no idea how long he's been at the college and what, if anything, he did before. He's a mysterious, wise man of mystery, and I like it that way.

Dr. Tenby's office is high on the fourth floor, next to the library. I knocked. 'Cam in.' I entered. He was standing next to the plinth and his '1914' globe, half-way between the window and the desk, dressed in a brown tweed suit.

I looked around keenly, knowing it was most likely my last time there. I loved the pictures on the walls, a mix of photos and prints, spanning all historical eras, from King Harold with an arrow in his eye, to Henry Kissenger talking on a phone, to the Soviet flag coming down on a snowy Moscow night, and the red, white and blue Russian one rising to take its place.

A touch of Dr. Tenby's veiny hand brought the spinning globe to a halt. A red, gigantic Germany stared up at me. Dr. Tenby didn't invite me to sit. He usually did. He just flicked his glasses up from his nose, stayed where he was, and cracked straight on. 'Young lady,' he began, 'you must understand that my chief concern is not your foolish choice to forego higher education when you could have graced any UK university, nor your adolescent stubbornness in refusing to make a deferred application. My anxiety, as I have previously suggested, revolves around the Head of this questionable establishment and the pseudo-mystique he dazzles gifted, but raw and impressionable young people with.'

He shook his woolly head. Sunlight streamed the room. 'Nah then, my dear, as I have told you before, there is no doubt in my mind that you are capable of becoming a first rate historian. You have an imaginative understanding of the Second World War, for example, that I have yet to encounter in anyone else, even in scholars three or four times your age. Take your essay on the Blitz, which I have just been re-reading – an outstanding exposition, both of the terror and the camaraderie engendered by that phenomenon.'

It was nice of him to say. I'd heard it all before though. I was sure I'd told him a million times. 'Thank you, Sir. I get all that from my Dad, Sir. Didn't I tell you? Just before he died, he showed me a picture-book: *Liverpool at War*. The piccies have stayed with me ever since. They feed my imagination. That's why I wrote about the Blitz, Sir, and how people pulled together in Liverpool, London and everywhere the Germans bombed. I'd love to know how it might have gone if the Germans had won and the country would've been occupied.

Dr. Tenby sighed. 'So do I, my dear. So do I.' Then, finally. 'Sit *dahn*, please.'

His desk was crammed with books and papers, stacked so high that once we were sat down I could only really see his head. 'Why spoil it then, Julie? Why waste your father's legacy on an individual who, it is apparent, has turned his back not only on the establishment that rejected him, but on modernity as a whole. Ambrosius Carlisle, from everything I hear, uses the Arts as a Trojan Horse to inaugurate some anti-rational, far-right simulacra of the Roman Empire. Do you think this is what your father would have wanted? To see your intellectual gifts deployed to such dubious ends?'

I had no answer, but the very next second Dr. Tenby's face brightened. He waved his hands about like he was shooing a crowd of pigeons. 'Of course, my dear, I have only met the man on the page, not in person. Mr. Martin knows him well, and Mr. Martin is a sound judge, both of books and people. My source lives in France. He is an economic forecaster. His perspective is necessarily limited. Perhaps he is a little, erm, out of the loop, as you young people say.'

He chuckled merrily. He'd made his point and was happy to gloss it over with laughter. The cunning devil. He asked about FACT, gave the same advice as Vivi, and went on about uni's for a bit: Glasgow, Bristol, Kings, etc. But I knew he'd meant what he said earlier, and that that was why he'd called me in.

I gave it no credence though. I'd no doubt that this 'source' – a dry as dust 'economic forecaster' – was eaten up with jealousy of Carlisle's creativity, originality and flair. And anyway, during the summer (I should say, by the way, that I received a note of acceptance from Mr. Carlisle in May) I'd conducted a little research of my own into things.

Constantine's Chambers does not, surprisingly, have its own website. Ambrosius Carlisle does not have one either. All that comes up when you search one or the other is a list of exhibitions and events held there, links to Carlisle's essays and articles (usually to do with Shakespeare or poets like Eliot and Yeats), and comments from former students. I looked at just one of these, from the painter, Rob Floyd. 'Ambrosius Carlisle,' he wrote, 'is the choice and master spirit of this age. Without his visionary, intuitive, soulful guidance, I would have been unable to complete my Stations of the Cross cycle, which, *Deo Gratias*, premiered so successfully at Manchester Cathedral this Lent and Easter.'

I also had this year's edition of the *Chlorian Review* to browse through, which had come (along with a little map of Didsbury) with the letter I received in May. It was a thick, nicely put together book of essays and reviews (many, but not all, by Ambrosius Carlisle) as well as accounts from the general public of plays and performances held at Constantine's Chambers. 'Truly transformative theatre,' wrote the brilliantly-named, Konstantin Kaidanovsky, of the Holy Grail reworking Mr. Martin had told me about. 'When, from the darkness of the chapel, the Grail procession appears, the impulse to fling oneself on one's knees, together with the actors, becomes well-nigh impossible to master.'

'What's not to like?' I remember thinking. Vivi and Dr. Tenby, God love 'em, could say what they wanted. I was busting a gut to get to Constantine's Chambers.

I'd only been to Manchester once before (not counting those childhood escapades when Dad used to whisk me away in his cab), the previous September, when Mr. Martin took us to see *The Tempest* at the Royal Exchange.

The theatre, I remember, was totally amazing – a space-pod style contraption with yellow girders shooting out like mechanical spider's legs. It stood in the middle of a spectacular, opulent hall. Massive pillars, washed and powdered in soft pink light, stretched up to the curves and arches of the cool blue ceiling. Magical, mystical domes of blue and white chequered glass – three in all – watched over and blessed us from above.

Mr. Martin, before the play, walked us around to the back of the hall. Characters glared out from gold-framed black and white photos high on the walls. A girl in a suit of armour with bright eyes and close-cropped spiky hair stood in the centre, fierce and proud on a wooden podium. 'Saint Joan,' said Mr. Martin's voice beside me. I looked up and nodded, though I didn't know who or what he meant. His eyes stayed focused on the photo as he spoke. 'You could be on that wall in my view one day, Julie. Not, perhaps, as an actor, but certainly as a writer. You have imagination and a natural sense of theatre; all one needs in essence to write for the stage.'

Then, before I'd time to take it in or think of a reply, Arabella Chung, that hyper-active ball of mischief, sprang out from behind a pillar, tugging at Mr. Martin's sleeve. 'Don't go giving her ideas, Sir,' she babbled. She's full of herself already. She calls herself the college bard, Sir.'

'I do no such thing.'

'She tells tales about goddesses singing.'

Bella leapt laughing at me, messing up my hair, then tripping me onto the deck. Back and forth we wrestled on the hard, gleaming floor. I didn't mind. I was happy, to be honest, to roll around for a while and have a giggle. Bella's silly and mad, but full of bounce and fun. Totally lacking in malice. Which was more than could be said, I felt, for the jeering Mancs watching on.

'Daft Scousers.'

'Can't take 'em anywhere.'

'Better 'em clownin' round than robbin', mind.'

Their cocksure tone repelled me. It made me feel sick, even as I turned the tables on Bella, pulling her ponytail until she pretended to yelp for mercy. It reminded me, strangely, of the Stations of the Cross in the Catholic Cathedral – those dramatic, intense, no-holds-barred, mini-statues – Christ's body all mashed up and broken – twisted, leering faces above, distorted with demonic, demented rage, as he lies there helpless and abandoned – fallen, for the third time, under the weight of the cross.

I pinched Bella on the cheek, but my mood had darkened. 'It's the same as with Christ,' I concluded, 'the same gobshites gozzing on his head and abusing him: fat, beer-bellied, loudmouth twats.'

****

The conductor – a Manc by the sound of him – swung by and clipped my ticket. His sky blue shirt flopped out over his trousers. He had sweatmarks under his arms as well.

I stretched my legs to the right. The seat beside me was free now. I hadn't even noticed the fella getting off. The train bulleted through Rainhill, then angled across a glimmering river that curved like the blade of an Arabic sword. A packed-out motorway followed. I felt I was leaving Liverpool further and further behind. I was missing it already. I knelt on the seat and tried to open the window, but the catch wouldn't budge and I had to sit back down.

The train flew across another motorway, accelerating towards Manchester at a million miles an hour. An ash-grey road ran parallel to the left. Lorries and cars pelted up and down. Terraced houses, high on the other side, looked on. Mancland was on me and I felt totally out of sorts, thrown off balance by the hostile, hard-edged buildings lining the route. Everything seemed so random and cluttered. Nothing like our Cathedrals to soften the view.

I could see, to my right, in what was probably once a factory or mill, a number of blokes, hot and bothered in shirts and ties, talking on phones and tapping on keyboards. To my left, a titanic skyscraper, the biggest of all time, gobbled up half the sky. All I could hear in my head was Billy's voice, over and over again: 'just a load of glass and steel, just a load of glass and steel …'

I stood up and hauled down my luggage. I was sorry I'd come now, and wondered if it might indeed still be possible to go back, live with Gina or (at a push) Bella, make peace with Billy, go back to FACT, etc. I walked down the aisle and stood by the door, wishing I was sat in the cool and dark of the Cathedral again, listening to the clip-clop of shoes and watching the tiny red squiggles wriggle into life on the stained-glass blue.

'We are now approaching Oxford Road,' the conductor announced. 'Manchester Oxford Road is the next station stop. Please mind the gap between the train and the platform edge.'

I pressed the button and opened the door. The crowd of pasty-faced Mancs jostled me from behind and hustled me off the train like there was no tomorrow.

Outside, I laid down my things, loosened the bandana a fraction and had a scan around. No welcoming committee, just stressball office types piling into the station. A wasp buzzed my left cheek. I swatted it away.

The street in front of me sloped down to the left, towards a Sainsbury's and a crazily busy road. Down there, somewhere to the right, so said my map, was the bus stop I needed for Didsbury and Constantine's Chambers.

Sunlight warmed my face. A nice-looking café, across the way, tempted me. People were sat outside smoking. But I picked up my stuff and walked forward instead, accidentally toe-ending a stone as I went. It bounced down the slope and cannoned off the front right tyre of a small orange bus coming into the station. The driver – a tough-looking guy with a scar on his chin – shook his head and scowled. Miserable bastard. I poked out my tongue, grabbed the stone, flung it up to the sun, closed my eyes and caught it with my left hand. Just like that. Easy peasy.

'Bards don't ever go back,' I remembered. 'Only forward.' But I *had* gone back. Back to the Queen of Liverpool, a brave and bold soldier girl, entering the enemy city this time, at the head of her very own army.

VIII

I'd found Grenfell Road easily enough after my bus ride – a thirty minute mega-mix of universities, parks, shisha bars and halls of residence – getting off at the white clock tower in the middle of Didsbury Village. The very first thing I saw (and heard) was a group of beery, bare-chested blokes – chanting, roaring and bellowing from outside a pub to my right.

One of them shouted something rude. I blushed, gripped my luggage tight, looked to my left (but not my right) and scrambled across the road, forcing a bus to brake in front of me with a whine and squeal of tyres. I walked on and kept my head down, too embarrassed to act cheeky and poke out my tongue again. The boozy laughter rang in my mind, but I was feeling too weary to turn back and start shouting the odds at the scuzzies. Another time.

I followed a paved, bendy pathway, with Didsbury Library to my right and a clump of trees bordered by a small green fence to my left. The library, to my eyes, had the air of a miniature Cathedral. Arches, domes and turrets gave the impression of a house of silence and grace. I made a mental note to pop across as soon as I could and have a proper peek inside.

I navigated another main road and carried on to the right. A church spire, its cross ornately patterned up on top, soared high into the sky. The ache in my arms subsided. A spring returned to my step. I passed four cafés, two estate agents and one electrical shop, before finding Grenfell Road, a narrow side-street to the left. Parked cars straggled onto the pavement and made it hard for me to get past, but the road made up for it in style with a gorgeous display of ivy-clad houses and technicolour flowers.

A long, uninterrupted terrace ran the length of the left hand side of the street. The properties had a certain Georgian or Regency vibe and looked quite similar, at first glance, to the houses I knew so well on Canning and Huskisson Streets. But it only took a second to nail them as fakes. The windows and roofs were far too shiny, far too new, for authentic L8 Georgian.

I crossed the road, bearing left past bigger, grander, Victorian-type gaffs. Rose-purple clematis clambered up, as if in welcome, from tiny pockets of garden, protected (not very well as far as the wasps and bees were concerned) by small black iron fences.

I counted eight doors before I came to Constantine's Chambers and dropped my suitcase and bag on the ground. Another terrace, identical in style to the one across the road, started up to the left of the building, but I'd no interest in other houses now. This was *the* house. Constantine's Chambers. And I, little Julie Carlton, was standing in front of it. Nothing in the whole wide world – no job, no university, no bunch of friends back home – could be better or more exciting than that. My one regret was that I'd had to honour my contract at FACT right up to yesterday, Tuesday 30th September, which meant I could only arrive on the Wednesday, the actual first day of term.

Handsome and imposing, the house towered above me, standing alone, huger by far than all the others on the road. I leant my arms on the little wall, lifted my head and studied my reflection – moonface, bandana, turned up collar – in the curvy bay window to the left of the red double-doors. Aside from a pair of white curtains, dragged back and tied at the middle with scarlet ribbons, I could see nothing inside at all. 'The light must be hitting the glass the wrong way,' I figured. Same with the right-hand window. Upstairs, and the floor above that, had two more bay windows, while three attic frames – built into the roof – capped off the house in white window triangles like the points of a crown.

I picked up my baggage and walked to the gate – a yellow affair with thin iron bars running down. A wooden placard hung from a green catch. ***Constantine's Chambers*** said the writing in rich red italics.

I swivelled around and pushed the gate open with my hip. A crunchy gravel path weaved through scented beds of dahlias, petunias, and green and white hydrangea plants towards the double-doors, the right of which, I noticed, lay slightly ajar.

I forced it open with my other hip and found myself standing in a cool stone porch, with a matching set of double-doors (but blue this time instead of red) straight ahead. The left-hand door had a painting in a delicate-looking, gold-leaf frame attached to it, about two thirds of the way up. I dropped my luggage on the floor and stepped forward for a better look.

Engraved in the wall, above the frame, were two capital letters – a P and an X – super-imposed on top of each other, to form a strange-looking symbol, about six inches high.

The painting itself was about the same size as an IPad screen. I couldn't make head nor tail of it at first. I thought it a shapeless (though colourful) mess. But the more I looked, the more the swoops, spirals and splashes started to make sense.

A jagged-branched tree stood on its own to the right. The sky was milkshake pink and gold, the sun – on the left – a fuzzy orange ball, while the rocks at the front glowed and throbbed in tawny, russet red.

Two figures, entwined together, dominated the scene, one nearly naked, the other in a purple robe and hood. A massive pair of wings unfurled up and out behind the pair, but I couldn't make out which of the two they belonged to.

Below the painting hung a small plaque, with writing in the same italic font:

And Jacob was left alone;
and there wrestled a man with him until the breaking of the day.

Still studying the picture and script, I tested the weight of the door with my hand. It gave way, to my surprise, and opened with a click, then a hiss, like it was sliding over thick carpet. I turned and booted my suitcase and bag into the gaff. Stepping over them, I stood with my hands on my hips, inspecting my new surroundings. I was standing in a long, high-ceilinged hallway. The carpet was orange (though thinner than I'd expected) and the walls beige. Brown doors faced each other at equal intervals. They all had that funny symbol carved into their wood. The hallway was bright, but not blindingly so. I thought it best to leave the doors behind me open. Just in case.

I inched forward. The door to my left was closed, but the one to my right stood a little open. I glimpsed an antique-looking book, with a red leather cover and gold lettering, leaning casually against the corner of a shelf. The smell of the old books drove me wild, transporting me back, on a magic carpet ride, to the St. Mark's library, high on the fourth floor, and hour after magical hour in the company of Prospero, King Arthur, Aslan, and the Celtic, Greek and Viking myths.

The next set of doors, to left and right, were closed. The end of the hallway came quicker than I expected, with a swish chandelier, then a stylish staircase with a shiny polished bannister, shooting up in a sharp diagonal to the right.

I stood beneath the chandelier. A short passageway branched off to the right. It had a red telephone – old-school style, with a round dial – half way up the wall at the end. A blue door next to it hung an inch or so ajar, letting a shaft of sunlight steal in through the gap. Bees buzzed outside, and I cottoned on to a totally gorgeous (though quite surprising) mix of smells – coffee to my right, along the passageway somewhere; and paint to my left, from the last room in the hallway. The door was open. I heard the splash-splash-splosh of paintbrush on canvas. So I crept up, stood at the side of the door, and peeped in.

A girl with wavy blonde hair was scrabbling around on the floor with a pile of brushes and a dozen or so clay pots. A giant window to the right with green rolled-back curtains gave me a view of the garden, the garage, the wall, and the chimney-tops of the houses on the next street. The artist wore jeans and a navy-blue sweater stained with yellow and red splodges. She looked a couple of years older than me. A gigantic work-in-progress lay on the floor beneath her, depicting a row of shops with a wall of golden sandbags a few metres in front. The artist bent over the canvas, her back arching like a cat's. She was lost in her work; unaware of my presence.

Three equally massive paintings leant against the wall directly facing me. Furthest left was a night scene – a row of slender poplars, with Georgian attics and rooftops poking up behind. The houses took me back, once again, to Canning Street and home, though unlike L8, and even the pretend efforts over the road, these windows had been completely stripped of every hint of life and light. Totally dismal. Waste and void. A wafer-thin moon in the top-left corner sprinkled the façades with a drizzle of dreary light.

A monumental building with a million shattered windows blazed in a riot of orange and black in the next canvas. It brought back to my mind Dad's book – *Liverpool at War* – and the photos of warehouses on fire at Herculaneum Dock. I scrunched up my eyes and spotted a faint lined pattern superimposed on the flames, a criss-cross mesh exposing a tissue of diamonds embedded in the texture of the painting's sizzling surface.

A mighty domed cathedral, crowned with a silver cross, bossed things on the canvas to the right. Smaller buildings – red, brown and gold – hung clustered around. A river meandered through the foreground. Men in flat caps stood on bridges and boats. The sun was a small flat disc.

I was totally hooked by the light in the picture, a light emanating not from the sun, but somehow from inside the painting itself. The artist, by hook or by crook, had woven it in to the fabric of her work – a strong, reflective radiance – pulsing its way through church and school, bank and shop, cathedral, sky and river.

I thought I saw, for a moment, the outline of a winged golden lion in the water. I leant forward, nearly lost my balance, steadied myself and shivered, as I felt the weight of a pair of eyes spying me from behind. I held my breath, spun on a sixpence, and beheld a tall, scholarly-looking bloke with a dark bushy beard standing right in front of me. A square felt hat, of a type I'd not seen before, sat fractionally skew-wiff on top of his head. He had round, John Lennon-style glasses, and his eyes were blue like diamonds. He was wearing a black robe with a red rope belt and brown shoes, which (if I'm being honest) could have done with a quick-fire polish.

I breathed out. Late-afternoon sun smashed through the still wide open inner and outer doors behind him, shining like a spotlight on my suitcase and bag. I could see the houses on the other side of the street. A guy with too much gel in his hair stood in a yellow doorway, fastening the cuffs of his off-white shirt and whistling a tune I couldn't hear. He disappeared inside, only to pop right back in a black, slightly too big, dinner jacket. He closed the door and turned right towards the main road. I wondered where he was going, then the man in the hat started talking and I forgot all about him.

'Good afternoon, Miss Carlton. It is a grace and benison to meet you. Thank you for choosing Constantine's Chambers.'

His voice was gentle, his accent posh, with no trace of Geordie, just a cute lisp, so when he said 'Miss Carlton', for instance, it came out as '*Mith* Carlton'.

'Thank you, Sir,' I said. And then, without knowing why: 'Are you a priest please, Sir?'

The man made no reply, just fixed me with his jewelbright eyes. I felt a stillness and serenity flowing out from him to me that filled me with a peace and sense of rest I'd never felt before.

'Are you a wizard then, Sir?'

Again no reply, just eyes like shafts of light.

'Or a king?'

He smiled, and it seemed to me, despite his beard, that something boyish, something playful, sparked into life on his face. His eyes danced.

'I am all these things, Miss Carlton. Or none, if you prefer. The world knows me as Ambrosius Carlisle. But here my name is Caesar. Augustus Ceasar. Welcome to Constantine's Chambers.'

IX

Not long after, I found myself following him up the stairs. He carried my bag in his left hand and my suitcase in his right. I was surprised, given his slim physique, by his suppleness and strength. He showed no sign whatsoever of discomfort or strain.

The mingled scent of coffee and paint faded and ebbed as we reached the first landing. Sunlight arrowed in through an arch-shaped window of tinted green and blue, skidding off the bannister and skimming the orange carpet. My lace came undone. I bent down to tie it. The filtered light was nice. It reminded me of happy trips with Gina (and Billy now and again) to Cheshire Oaks and the *Blue Planet* aquarium.

The staircase continued. I glanced down – the window behind me now – at the hallway and lower flight of stairs. We emerged onto a short wide corridor. Carlisle turned left, into a longer, thinner passageway, then left again, into a spacious, sun-dappled chamber. A massive bay window looked out onto the terrace opposite. A street I hadn't noticed before, a little to the left, cut the row of neat and tidy houses in two.

'Take a seat,' he said, as he popped down my stuff in the middle of the room beside a tasselled Persian carpet. I remember how impressed I was by its interlocking, interweaving mesh of green and purple squares and circles.

Plain unvarnished floorboards surrounded it, with a chunky round table of brown mahogany filling the space between the carpet and the window. Two ordinary-looking wooden chairs slotted neatly under the table, across the carpet in front of me, while a more elaborate specimen, replete with velvet armrests, regarded me snootily from the further side.

I'd nearly stepped across the carpet to pull back one of the chairs when I spotted the sofa to my right. It was green and had three white cushions – one in the middle, one on the left and one to the right. The same design featured on each – a flowing black line, like the stem of a flower, with three intertwining circles at the top. I walked over and sat on the sofa's edge, my right hand fiddling with the middle cushion, as I scanned the room from top to bottom.

The opposite wall was crammed from ceiling to floor with books. I widened my eyes as wide as I could, but no matter how hard I tried, I couldn't make out the titles or even the type of literature lining the shelves. And that was when I realised that my host was no longer with me. Where'd he gone? I looked at the door. It was shut. I scrunched up my eyes and thought really hard, but couldn't recall when the door had been closed or by whom.

The door, I might as well say, was as green as the sofa, with the ceiling and walls a soft, restful purple. Neither art nor ornament (apart from the carpet and cushions) could be seen anywhere in the room, but that didn't detract from the cultured, scholarly vibe. Not at all. The view from the window, in fact, was just like looking at a proper painting. Rooftops, chimneys, telegraph wires and aerials bristled with clarity and distinction.

Then the door, with a rasp and a squeak, opened to my left. I turned my head, and Ambrosius Carlisle (or Augustus Ceasar) was back, gliding over the threshold with a glass of water in each hand.

'So that's why the door was shut,' I decided. 'He must have slipped out while I was looking at the carpet. How strange I never noticed. Maybe he really is a wizard after all.'

I went to run her hand through my hair, as was my habit, but stopped when I realised I couldn't because I had the bandana on. My hand hovered uncertainly. But not for long. Carlisle handed me a glass. 'Drink,' he said. 'You are tired and thirsty.'

I took a sip. The water was delicious – clear and crisp – more like light than liquid. He closed the door, came back, and stood beside me as I drank.

'Thank you, Sir. The water's lovely.'

'Caesar,' he replied. 'My students call me Caesar.'

'Ceasar, Sir?'

'That's right, Miss Carlton. Caesar.' He joined his hands together, like he was saying a prayer or conducting a ceremony. Dr. Tenby's warning reverberated in my mind. But the more Caesar explained himself (I'll call him by his proper name from now on) the more I believed him and the more I resonated with him. He looked at me while he was speaking, you see, like I was the only person, or at least the most important person, in the whole wide world.

'There has to be a hierarchy,' he went on. 'There needs to be a hierarchy. Especially here at Constantine's Chambers. Hierarchy is our very *raison d'être*.'

He turned around, stepped over my luggage, walked across the carpet and stood in front of the table, taking off his hat and laying it down on the mahogany. There it sat, in a widening slice of shade, like a watchful, wary cat. Caesar's hair, I observed, was brown like his beard, but shorter, with a little bald patch at the crown. He was looking at the carpet now, hands behind his back, casting a spell, I imagined, on the circles and squares. I finished my water, crossed my right leg over my left, let go of the cushion, and ran my finger around the glass's rim. Caesar lifted his head, looked across at me and carried on where he'd left off.

'Hierarchy, as you will be aware from your college studies, does not have to be oppressive. Authority is not in itself restrictive. *Au contraire*, it is the false creed of egalitarianism – the diktat that everyone and everything possesses equal intrinsic value – that represents the definition of oppression and stagnation. In a well-ordered polity, Miss Carlton, you will find monarchy working in concert with individuals of all ranks and stations towards the fulfilment of every person's unique vocation. The individual, as a result, is happy and settled, having located his or her proper place in society. To the artist, the canvas and brush. To the builder, the bricks and mortar. One no longer torments oneself with restless searching. One is no longer paralysed with uncertainty regarding who one is and what actions one ought, or ought not, to perform in the world.'

He thrust out his palm, as if in warning. 'To achieve this state, however, both at the individual and collective levels, is far from easy. One has to become king or queen of oneself. One has to wage war – war with oneself, Miss Carlton – in that fierce internal battle the Muslims know as the Greater Jihad. *Ecoute*.'

He whipped out a book from the depths of his robe; small and thick with a maroon cover. He leafed through it, found his place and began to read out loud, quietly but clearly, pausing a little at the end of each sentence:

'That night Jacob arose and took his two wives, his two maids and eleven children and crossed the ford Jabbok. He took them and sent them across the stream, and likewise everything that he had. Then Jacob was alone. A man came and wrestled with him until daybreak. When the man saw that he did not prevail, he struck Jacob on the hip socket, and Jacob's hip was put out of joint. Then the man said, 'Let me go, for the day breaketh.' Jacob replied, 'I will not let you go unless you bless me.' So the man asked, 'What is your name?' And he said, 'Jacob.' Then said the man, 'You shall no longer be called Jacob, but Israel, for you have wrestled with the divine and the human and have overcome.' Then Jacob asked, 'What is your name?' But the man said, 'Why do you ask my name?' And he blessed him, and Jacob called the place Peniel, saying, 'I have seen God face to face, and my life is preserved.'

Caesar closed his book. He stood, as before – eyes on the carpet, hands behind his back – like I might have imagined it all and he hadn't actually uttered a word. I gripped my cushion again and squeezed. The squidgy soft stuff fell and folded inwards, then bounced back up as I my hand let go. I looked at the marks my fingers were making. In and out they went like waves.

Caesar sat down on top of the table, next to his hat. I saw beneath his robe. He was wearing black kecks with a built-in turn up and grey cotton socks. A multi-coloured ball had appeared, while I was absorbed with the cushion, in his right hand, about half the size of a football, with patches of blue in the middle, and two white blobs – one at the top and one at the bottom. Caesar held it up to his face. I knew what it was – a globe of the world – but different in size and style from the globe I knew best, thirty-five miles away in Dr. Tenby's office. That globe was hard and firm. This was soft and squishy. Caesar squeezed it in and out as he spoke.

'That story, Miss Carlton, illustrates to a *t* exactly what Constantine's Chambers is about. Success and failure, as the world understands them, are irrelevant here. Encounter and engagement are our master words. We keep our appointment with the angel. We earn our blessing. That is all. Any art born from this contest is God's work alone.'

I uncrossed my legs and sat forward again.

'You are a student of *Macbeth*,' he continued, his attention still fixed on the globe. 'As am I, of course. But you have the edge in that you have written imaginatively, while I remain cabinned, cribbed and confined in the narrow parameters set by academia.'

I smiled. I liked that. He shrugged. 'We will say more about your work at dinner, but for now, Miss Carlton, meditate on this. A king is killed, a usurper claims the throne, and then, when darkness seems enthroned forever, the crown is wrested from his bloody head and a new sovereign, in the spirit and lineage of the old, assumes the purple and restores the ancient harmony.'

He lowered his arm and turned to face me. 'The king, it appears, has endured a fatal wound. But appearances, *Mith* Carlton, are deceptive. The king is not dead, merely sleeping, He sleeps, he dreams, he stirs, he wakes, and shatters the chains that bind. The Empire, as in the days of Augustus, will rise like the Phoenix, with the imagination once again playing its pre-ordained, pivotal role in the great dance between the human and divine. Augustus had Virgil for his bard, and the Aeneid as his *chef d'oeuvre*. Who will be the Virgil for our era, I wonder? The time for his or her advent, I sense, is close at hand.'

He slid down from the table and stood as before in front of the carpet, squeezing his globe again. The light outside, I noticed, was beginning to fade. The sky was a rich, expressive blue still, but it wouldn't be long, I could tell, before the moon and the stars started staking their claim.

'All this, I used to think, lies far in the future, long after you and I and everyone at Constantine's Chambers has passed on. Now I am not so sure. The world waxes old. Centrifugal forces are at work. "Things fall apart," wrote Yeats. "The centre cannot hold. Surely, some revelation is at hand. Surely, the second coming is at hand."'

He threw up the globe, half-way to the ceiling, and caught it in his right hand. 'But that,' he continued more cheerfully, 'is of little account right now. What counts, Miss Carlton, this very instant, is that we play our part. That is what matters. And that, in so many words, is what Constantine's Chambers is all about.'

I nodded and looked at his hat. It was blacker and sleeker, more like a curled-up sleeping cat than the wakeful sentry I'd imagined before. Then he foxed me – flinging the globe at my face with no warning or backlift. It bulleted through the air, but I put up my hands without thinking and caught it with ease. It was a sinch. Second nature. Easy peasy.

The globe felt like rubber in my hands. I wanted to throw it on the carpet and see how high it'd bounce, but Europe grabbed my attention, a coat of many colours, curving around on the side of the globe – France blue, Germany yellow, Italy red, Russia orange. And Caesar's voice came to me again:

'And Jacob went out from Beersheba and went towards Haran. And he lighted on a certain place, and tarried there the night, because the sun was set. And he took the stones of that place, and put them for his pillows, and lay down in that place to sleep. And he dreamed, and behold a ladder set up on the earth, and the top of it reached to Heaven: and behold the angels of God ascending and descending on the ladder.'

My eyes flashed back to the globe and the black squares marking Paris, Berlin, Moscow and Rome. I crossed the English Channel. Britain was green, like the sofa and door, but neither Liverpool nor Manchester appeared on the map, only London and

Edinburgh. But I didn't mind. I felt so happy. So excited. Then, suddenly, everything caught up with me. I fell asleep and dreamed of the moon and the stars and a brown polished ladder stretching from earth to Heaven and back again, with angels darting up and down with yellow wings and diamond-patterned robes of orange, red and blue.

X

The door was small, arch-shaped, and made from a dark, slightly bruised-looking wood. The key was small and golden. Caesar turned it in the lock, then handed it to me. 'Welcome, Miss Carlton, to your chamber.' The overhead light whirred into life. It had a big white shade and was as round as a ball. 'I hope that it fires your imagination.'

'Thank you, Sir. Th-th-thank you, Caesar, I mean.'

He patted my shoulder and laughed. 'You've got a stutter and I've got a *lithp*. It's an omen. We'll work well together, mark my words.' He picked up my things again, plonked them down, turned around and left me to it. 'We dine at eight tonight,' was his parting remark.

I closed the door and looked around. A narrow, white-framed window, with open orange curtains and a triangular pointy bit at the top, faced me. I bobbed across to the wooden desk (and chair) in front of it and flicked on the table-lamp. Now I had two lights going – one shining down, one beaming across – but it was the outside world that caught my imagination, especially the church spire with the fancy patterned cross I'd walked past earlier. I pulled back the chair, sat down, leant forward and craned my neck to the left. The spire was tall and thin – a needlepoint – jabbing up from earth to Heaven. I felt made up to see it there, like I'd a friend and comforter (I didn't want to say 'Guardian Angel' again) watching over my Constantine's Chambers adventure.

I got up, unwound my headband, turned off the big light and cracked on with the unpacking, unloading my gear into the wardrobe and drawers. The wardrobe was a hefty beast, next to the door, just to the right as you entered the room. The drawers stood on their own, half-way along the right-hand wall, with the bed lying opposite, its pillows and sheets white, crisp and immaculately-ironed. Next to its curvy grey plastic head came a little table, like you get in hotels, with a kettle, tea-bags, coffee and cups. Then, to the right, the window, desk and chair, with two bookshelves – one on top of the other – between the desk and right-hand wall. The walls were a warm, cosy blend of orange and red.

The wardrobe had lots of hangers running along the rail, which was just as well as I'd forgotten to bring any. As I was hanging my jackets and dresses, I noticed a few garments wedged together on the right. I took a couple out and had a gander. They were short-sleeved tunics. Seven in total. I'm wearing one now, in fact – the white one with the purple diamond sewn onto the front. There was a dark blue one with a yellow square, a red one with a golden star, a grey one with a yellow triangle, a brown one with a cream cross, a pale blue one with an orange sun-like ball, and a green one with a silver circle. I didn't try any of them on, but I could tell by their size and shape that they'd fit me perfectly. There were seven belts of rope as well in purple, green, yellow, red, grey, blue and gold.

I wasn't sure what I was meant to do with them all, so I did the next best thing and forgot all about them, turning my attention to the bookshelves.

I hadn't actually brought that many books with me, which was handy again, as there was less space to display them than I'd expected. I had all seven Narnia books, of course, as well as Roger Lancelyn Green's, *Tales of King Arthur.* I'd brought some A Level texts too: *The Wasteland* and *Waiting for Godot* plus *Richard II* and *Macbeth.* I couldn't go anywhere without Rosemary Sutcliff's Roman stories: *The Eagle of the Ninth, The Silver Branch* and *The Lantern Bearers.* Then, finally, the wartime stuff: *The Heat of the Day*, a novel by Elizabeth Bowen set in London, and Dad's *Liverpool at War* picture-book.

I'd also brought *Ulysses* by James Joyce. Mr. Martin said once that I should challenge myself by reading something different, so I chose *Ulysses*, because I knew it was to do with myth. So, in reality, I hadn't challenged myself at all, but it was certainly different in style – by a million, million miles – to anything I'd read before.

I'm not sure, now that I think of it, if I actually like it or not. Not a lot seems to happen, but some of the writing's fantastic. The way he runs words together and creates new ones makes me buzz, and I love the way he makes ordinary things – tables, chairs, plates, dogs, cats, etc, – so deep and holy and full of meaning. I'll give you my favourite passage so far:

Mr Bloom watched curiously, kindly, the lithe black form. Clean to see: the gloss of her sleek hide, the white button under the butt of her tail, the green flashing eyes. He bent down to her, his hands on his knees.

- Milk for the pussens, he said.

- Mrkgnao! the cat cried.

See what I mean?

I walked back to the desk, leant across and pulled closed the curtains. I couldn't see a mirror anywhere, so I dived into the top drawer and pulled out my trusty, pink-framed compact. It was my very first evening in Constantine's Chambers and I was determined to set about things in style. I grabbed my bath bits and bobs, nipped out of the room and scampered down the corridor to the shower area. A whole year of trekking to and from the toilet and shower wasn't quite what I had in mind when I applied, but still, the shower was hot, splurgy and nice. Easy to use as well. I was dreading getting muddled up with the taps and having to go and find someone to help. I wouldn't have known where to go. I didn't see or hear anyone. The corridor was dead dead quiet and the two doors between me and the shower (both to the right) were shut with no sign of presence or light.

When I was done, I went back to the wardrobe and thumbed through my dresses, opting in the end for the nifty '20s imitation – cream with lovely black trimmings – I'd picked up on Bold Street last year. I sat down at the desk, stood the little mirror up, twisted a few strands of black glossy hair, took up the ends, pinned them in place and fixed them with rapid-fire mists of hairspray. I squeezed some foundation onto my hand and dabbed it over my face with a small brush. I saw that spot on my chin I'd been trying to forget and nailed it with my concealer.

I went back to the wardrobe and pulled out my phone from my jeans pocket where I'd left it. *19:25*. Bags of time.

I gave my eye-lids a subtle touch of pencil, flicking up to the eyebrows. Then I took my lip-pencil out, lining my lips in a fire-engine red, taking great care with the 'm' at the top. I stood up and held out the mirror, unravelling the twists in my hair and running my fingers through to build volume. I took a fine tooth-comb and ran it down the side of my head, sweeping the hair across to the left and over my ear, gathering what was left into a small ponytail. I tied it with a black band, grabbed my black and white evening bag, stuffed my Rizlas and baccy in, splashed some *Eternity* about, stumbled into my high-heels, slung my black cardigan over my shoulders and glanced at my phone. "Still a few minutes to go. I'll have a look at those paintings again. She won't be there now. She'll be in her room getting ready like me.'

Before I went out though, I spotted something I'd not seen before – a little painting on the wall, just above the bed. How had I missed it? Its colours were simple and bold – silver, gold and red – and it looked totally ancient, like it had been painted in Medieval times or even before.

A woman with long silver hair knelt on the ground, arms open in welcome, the towers and turrets of a city behind her, the word LON written in the sky above her. A man in gold walked towards her from the sea, disembarking from a ship choc-a-bloc with soldiers and sailors, hung with numberless banners and shields. Above the man's head were three more words: REDDITOR LUCIS AETERNAE.

I hadn't taken Latin at St. Mark's. 'Something Light Eternal,' I guessed, before checking the time once more. *19:40*. Time to go time. Go, Jules, go…

I ran down the stairs two at a time till I reached the studio door. The paintsmell smacked me between the eyes. The light was on too. Yay! I'd nearly bowled straight in when I saw the artist still there, crouched over the sandbags and shops like time had totally frozen.

'Hi,' I said, carried away by my own momentum.

The artist turned, saw me and smiled. 'Hi,' she said, and there was a warmth and softness to her person that set me straight at ease. She stood up, wiped her hands on a brown rag, and walked across. She shook my hand. 'You must be Julie,' she said. 'I'm Claire. Good to meet you.' Her eyes were grey, her face long and her nose very straight. She looked a bit like a horse, I thought. A nice horse though.

She led me to the middle of the room, then skipped over to the left a second, coming back with a wooden crate. 'Take a seat,' she said, so I did, crossing my right leg over my left, as I sat on the splintery wood. I glanced to my left. The curtains were drawn. Claire sat cross-legged on the floor in front of me like a supple blonde Buddha.

I wasn't fully looking at her, to be honest, though. Her paintings, once again, were blowing me away. 'Your paintings are amazing,' was all I could say.

'Thank you,' she said, with a smile and a blush.

'Where are you from?"

'Portsmouth.'

I nodded my head, like I knew just where Portsmouth was, even though I hadn't a clue.

'That's where I started to paint, 'she said. 'So much water, so many waves, in and out, always shifting, never still. There's a lighthouse reflecting the sea, all the way across the harbour. It's amazing. You should see it. I've tried to paint it so many times, but I've never got it right.'

There was a dreamy, contemplative glint in her eyes, way down, like a buried gemstone, that I found most attractive. Words stopped for a while. They weren't needed.

'Do you think you'll get it right here? I whispered at length. 'Is that why you've come?'

'I'm not sure I'll ever get it right,' she replied. The magic spark spluttered, dimmed and went out. She bowed her head.

'You stupid, stupid girl,' I scolded myself. 'You shouldn't have asked that. You've made her all sad.'

'I'm here for the same reason as everyone else,' she carried on after a bit, still looking down. 'To have a break, try something different, take a year out before real life begins: money, family, career. That's the real world, innit? I'm just trying to put it off as long as I can. I think Caesar still is, between you and me.'

She looked up and laughed like a tinkling little bell. Her eyes glimmered. Her sadness had passed. As easy as that. But I was sad by what she had said. It distressed me how an artist of such class could get sucked down by all that 'real world' baloney.

'I've not thought of any of them things,' I said. 'Nor should you. Serious, Claire. Life's more than that. It's an adventure. A drama.'

I stood up, loosened my bag from my shoulder and watched it fall to the floor. 'You know what my English teacher says? Mr. Martin's his name. "Life is no dream," he says, "but it could and should become one." It was a German poet who said that. I've forgotten which one, but I know that it's true. I want to make it happen. I'm going to make it happen. I swear. That's why I'm here. And so are you, Claire. You're going to make it happen too. That's why *you're* here.'

Claire grinned and twiddled her hair. I sat back down, knackered, my burst of passion spent.

'You're brilliant,' she said. 'So charismatic. I can see why Caesar signed you up. You've a way with words, for sure. But you look very young, if you don't mind me saying. Are you still at uni?

'Not even started. I could have gone, but didn't want to. I wanted to come here instead. I've come straight from college. What about you?'

'Sussex.' She smiled, as if remembering something nice. 'Brighton's a wicked city. So much going on. You been?'

'No.' I didn't know where Brighton was either.

'But I'd had my fill of it. Too many hipsters. They wound me up. Got under my skin. I wanted to do something totally the opposite, something highbrow, a bit uncool, a bit un-PC. Know what I mean?'

I didn't really, but I nodded anyway. I liked the sound of her voice.

'So there you are,' she concluded. 'My tutor told me about this place, I applied, and here I am.'

'Me too,' I giggled. 'Caesar seems to know a lot of teachers.'

'He certainly does.' Claire inspected her watch. 'It's nearly time,' she said, flipping out of her 'lotus' with ease. 'We'd better be off.'

I stood up too, but Claire didn't actually seem to be in too much of a hurry to leave. She pointed to the burning-building painting. 'I started this suite in March,' she said. 'Ages ago now. But it fits like a glove with what Caesar wants us to do.'

'*Us?*' Does that mean the whole community or just you and me?'

'You and me, Julie. We've got what he calls a watching brief this term, while the actors put on *Macbeth*.'

'*Macbeth*. Wow.'

'That'll be the December revue. While they're doing that, we're supposed to develop a story – that'll be you – and create a bit of scenery – that'll be me – for the March revue.'

'What about?'

'King Arthur's return.' She paused. 'To a Nazi-occupied Britain.'

Hat trick! *Macbeth,* King Arthur, the war. How about that? Buzz buzz buzz went my heart and head like a pair of buzzy little bees.

'The actors'll act it out,' said Claire. 'That'll be the plan.'

'They seem a lot busier than us, the actors.'

'Oh no. It all works out the same. In the third term, you see, you and me have to write, paint *and* act.'

'Blimey.'

Claire walked to the door. I picked up my bag, slipped it back on my shoulder and followed. I spotted a little bowl, like a Holy Water stoup, cut into the wall by the door. 'Is Caesar a monk of some kind?' I asked. 'I mean, this place used to be a monastery, didn't it?'

Claire turned off the light and closed the door. We stood together under the chandelier. Fish was being cooked. I could smell it. Along the passageway. Same direction as the coffee before.

'They were called Chlorians,' said Claire. 'Did you know that?'

'Who?'

'The monks.'

'Chlorians?'

'Chlorians. After the Emperor, Constantius Chlorus. He brought Britain back to the Empire, Caesar says, after a usurper had taken it over. There's a picture in all our rooms. The same one. Constantius entering London. You seen it yet?'

I clicked my fingers. 'Oh yes, Constantius. I remember. He's in *The Silver Branch*, by Rosemary Sutcliff. You read that one?'

Claire laughed and shook her head. 'Nah. This is all stuff that Caesar said. At dinner last night. Constantius was the father of Constantine the Great, you know, the first Christian Emperor. That's why this house is called Constantine's Chambers, and that's Constantine's symbol on all the doors, the P and X joined together.'

'What happened to the monks?' I asked, still curious. 'Where'd they go?'

Claire shrugged. 'Dunno. Just grew old. Died out. Caesar says he's the last of them, so yeah, I guess he must be a monk. He's only the last in Britain, mind. There's more Chlorians abroad.'

'What does it say on the painting? Above the Emperor's head. Redditor something.'

'Redditor Lucis Aeternae. Restorer of the Eternal Light.'

'Ah, I wasn't far off.'

'That's what Chlorians worship, apparently. The light. Not Jesus, or not the Jesus the churches go on about anyway. The light of Rome, Caesar calls it. The eternal, ancient light. Roma Principia.'

I was only half listening. Something odd and perplexing had distracted me.

'What's that door?' I asked.

XI

'What door?

'That door.' I pointed to a brown wooden door between the staircase and the studio wall.'

'Dunno. A cleaning cupboard or something.'

'It wasn't there this afternoon. When I came in.'

'It must have been. You probably didn't see it.'

'I definitely didn't see it. It wasn't there, that's why.'

'Oh, come on, Julie. Of course it was there.'

'Was it? Have *you* seen it? Before now, I mean.'

'Every day.'

'How many?'

'Five.'

'Have you gone in?'

'No. Why should I? It's just a random door.'

'It wasn't here, Claire. I swear to God it wasn't.'

She stroked my arm. Her voice was soft and sympathetic. 'Come on, Julie. We'll be late. You've had a long day. It's a big thing, you know, coming here. It's a powerful place. Takes your breath away. Plays tricks with your mind.'

I walked across to the disputed door, foxed and befuddled. I was sure I hadn't seen it, sure it hadn't been there, sure I hadn't (on this occasion) been imagining things. I looked at Constantine's symbol, said a silent prayer to it and turned the knob. The door clicked. I pushed it open, and lo and behold, a spiral stone staircase swooped down clockwise before me. I could see just the first five steps before darkness swallowed them up. I turned back to Claire. 'Well, well, well,' I said. I unzipped my bag and rooted around for my lighter. I wanted it so I could see, but a sixth sense told me I shouldn't, so I took out my phone instead and held it up in front of me. Claire was standing beside me now, eyes focused on the steps, but palefaced in the extreme, a Buddha no more.

'Fancy a look?' I said.

'I'm game if you are,' she replied, though she looked more scared than thrilled. I no longer, I realised, felt younger than her. Quite the reverse. I felt older now. Much older.

The stairway was narrow and steep. The phone's little beam shone only a metre or two ahead. I had to keep pressing the screen to keep the gleam going. The air was cool; the turns tight and twisting. High heels clattered on stone.

'Are we nearly there yet?' said Claire. Her whingey tone annoyed me.

'It's my first day, Claire. How'm I supposed to know how long it goes for?'

'It might go on for ever.'

She sounded scared. I was too. I tried to hide it. 'Do you want to go back?' I said.

'No,' came the sulky reply.

We carried on in silence.

'There's something there,' said Claire, after a while. 'At the bottom. Getting bigger. Can you see?'

'No.'

'There. Look.'

I shook my head. 'Maybe it'll come clear in a bit.'

'We must be miles down. We'll definitely miss dinner now.'

Then I saw it – a tiny golden glimmer creeping around the corners.

'I've got it, Claire. I can see it.'

'Good,' said Claire. 'We'll soon be there.'

'Good?' I queried. 'We don't know what it is. It might be a fire or a trap.'

I pressed the screen again. A door slammed shut high above. The lock turned and echoed. We looked at each other.

'Come on,' I said, with fake composure. 'Let's see what's here. It might be a way out for all we know.'

The sense of time started to shake and slide in my mind. How long had we been down there? Five minutes? Five hours? I'd absolutely no idea. I began to imagine there might be something hiding in the walls, biding its time before pouncing, or that my foot might kick against something slimy and horrid, something alive, or – worse – something dead.

The golden glow grew brighter. Soon we didn't need the phone. We turned another bend and stumbled out onto flat, crumbly ground. We looked around. We were in a hollowed-out chamber made from big stone blocks, lit by a massive burning brazier attached to the wall to our right. Straight ahead was a steep stone stairway – straight not spiral. To our left was a small chapel, framed by a rough uneven archway. We crept close. There were six wooden pews, three on either side of a narrow central aisle. At the end was an altar, with a little stone door behind it to the left. To the right, fixed to the wall with bronze hooks, was a golden spear with a red tip. I couldn't believe it. Nor could I believe the silver sword and chunk of lumpy rock – about the size of a football – lying on the floor in front of the altar.

Two candles burned on the barestone altar, one to the left and one to the right. A small golden bookstand stood between them in the centre. I couldn't see anything on it from where I stood, but I knew I felt compelled to go and look. I was convinced, on a deepdown level, that, as with Dad's Bridget story, there was something there – a book most likely – directly to do with me. I was determined not to miss my moment again.

'Come on,' I whispered. 'Let's have a shufty.'

We walked stealthily up the aisle, then around to the back of the altar. Claire squeezed my hand. 'Do you think we should?' she said.

'We must,' I said, in a voice that seemed no longer mine. Not 'little Julie' anyway. This was an older me, as I'd already sensed – bigger, deeper, wider – 'St. Mark's Julie', more like – but somehow younger as well, like at one and the same time I'd become older *and* younger than the world I lived in. It was a most peculiar sensation.

I was as nervous as anything though, miles more nervous than I let on. I was standing on the wrong side of the altar, you see. Everything in my upbringing told me so. At any moment a cloud of holy light might appear and blast me to cinders for trespassing on holy ground. But the inner command was too strong. This was my moment. I had to see what was there.

It was a paperback, about half the size of an Ipad. The title, *Constantine's Chambers*, was written in a red sweeping font, standing out boldly against a starry nightsky backdrop. Below was a lifelike drawing of the building itself, lights blazing out in every room, with little knots of people standing together, chatting and smoking, on the street outside. Everything looked realistic and bang up to date. I saw a girl in a fashionable quilted navy shawl, for instance, and a guy with a black and white Adidas sports bag that looked a lot like mine except smaller.

I turned the page. There were no words, just a picture – a girl with dark hair holding something bright and round in her hands. What was it? I'd no idea. A ball? A globe? A model sun or moon? A big building stood behind her, like a church or Cathedral.

'That's you,' said Claire. She touched my hair. I shook my head. I wasn't sure. I bent my head to get a better look, then heard a key turn to my right, and a door creak open. I stood up straight and gripped Claire's hand. Caesar stood before us in a white robe with purple trimming at the neck and cuffs. A golden circlet ran through his bushy brown hair. His glasses were gone, and in his hands he held a silver chalice, the brightest thing I've ever seen. His eyes were

jets of hot blue sapphire fire. I was out of my depth, and knew it –
straying into some timeless, holy scene – crossing the line between
'Planet Julie' and the sacred sphere of wizards, priests and kings.
The wrong side of the altar.

'Christ Almighty. Leg it.'

And we did, hand in hand, out of the chapel, to the left this
time, up the straight stone stairs. Clatter clatter clatter. I'd no idea if
Caesar was after us. No way was I going to look back. Our hands
split apart. Claire pulled ahead, her loping stride making short work
of the staircase. 'Light straight ahead,' she called down.

'Giz a sec,' I panted.

I joined her at the top. In front of us was a door. Light winked
at us from the top, bottom and sides. I was so out of puff that I pretty
much collapsed right against it. It's easier running down stairs than
up, let me tell you. The door fell open and we tumbled inelegantly
through, into what looked like a small Medieval refectory. Five men
and women sat at a round table stood up as one and gawped at us
like we'd been catapulted at from the dark side of the moon.

I could smell fish again. Cod, I was sure.

XII

It was a big fella in a green shirt – a livewire, jack-in-the-box type – who spoke first. He had a bald head and wore a roll-neck jumper very much like Mr. Martin's (though black instead of blue). He smiled at my new friend. 'Good evening, Claire,' he said, then turned to me. 'You must be Julie. Welcome to Constantine's Chambers.' He spoke in a Scottish accent. 'So now, if my Maths are correct, which they very rarely are, I think that makes our company complete.'

He walked around the table. We shook hands.

'I'm Jim,' he said. 'I act.' He glanced back at the table, as if for support. 'And sometimes risk my professional standing by dabbling in a little poetry.' I think he thought they'd laugh, but no-one did. They just smiled, like he cracked the same joke every night. Then they introduced themselves to me, one by one, anti-clockwise around the table: 'Hi, I'm Camilla', 'Philip', 'Jacqueline', 'Jean-Luc'.

'H-h-hi everyone,' was all I could muster in reply, as I waved embarrassedly.

Jean-Luc, a tall, African-looking guy in a white, super-bright robe, pulled back a chair and nodded at me. I sat down beside him, on the left of the table from the way we'd come in. The girl called Jaqueline – a haughty-looking brunette, with bunned-up hair and black-rimmed glasses – was sat to my right. Claire, once she'd shut the staircase door, faced me from the other side, between Philip and Camilla. Philip wore a green shirt with a white sweater tied around his neck. His face was pale; his hair dark. He had a habit of biting his nails.

Camilla, with her flowing locks and elfin bone structure reminded me in some ways of Vivi, but in other ways not at all. She used to waif around the place with such a bored, listless look on her face – a million miles from Vivi's bounce and fire – like she'd declared herself too cool for life and had decided just to bat out time till she died.

We all had a glass of water in front of us. I took a sip and felt instantly refreshed.

'Did you get a bit of a shock then?' Jim piped up. 'I can tell by your faces you did. You must have disturbed Caesar at work.'

Claire leant forward, curtain-like hair flopping over her eyes. 'Did any of you know,' she asked in hushed tones, addressing the whole table and (it seemed to me) studiously ignoring Jim, 'that there's a spiral staircase running down to the basement from the door between the stairs and the studio?'

'Really?' asked Jean-Luc, with a bassline chuckle. 'How romantic. How mysterious. Like a device from a gothic novel. How did you discover it?'

'The door was open,' Claire continued, totally recovered and composed, like she was telling the story just as it happened, even though she wasn't. 'So we saw the stairs and went down. Just for a bit of adventure, y'know.'

'It leads to the mock-theatre, I take it,' interjected Jim with lively eyes. I bit my bottom lip. That was an insult. Whatever we'd stumbled on downstairs was a million times more sacred, strange and holy than a 'mock theatre'.

Claire sat back, folded her arms, and took her time before carrying on, like she didn't want to give him the satisfaction of replying instantly. 'Indeed it does,' she said at length. 'Caesar *was* there. And he *was* at work – acting out a ritual of some kind. He was so wrapped up that he didn't see us at all. So we sneaked past him, up these stairs, and here we are.'

'Phew,' said Jim, his wispy eyebrows raised. 'You've had a lucky escape and no mistake. When he had us upstairs in the Drama Space yesterday – Camilla, Philip, Jean-Luc and I – he gave us strict orders never to go down there without him. "It's my own private workspace," he said. He took us down for a look, but this was the door we used. I'd no idea there was a door in the hall. Poor old Lolek'll get it in the neck, that's for sure.'

Then, as if on cue, another door opened, straight ahead of me, on the left side of the facing wall. A man with brown curly hair, wearing a black shirt and trousers, came in backways, dragging behind him a silver trolley, laden with pots, bowls, spoons, plates and knives. This was my first sight of 'poor old' Lolek.

'Soup's up,' Jim called out heartily. Everyone stood up and headed over to the trolley. One by one we poured our soup, then cut and buttered a slice or two of granary bread. Lolek, meanwhile, had disappeared the way he'd come. He was a plump, round-faced bloke, and I liked him straightaway.

The soup was thick and salty with carrots, sweet potato, and peppers-a-plenty. I was glad it was nice, glad of the fish smell as well, because I was finding it hard to get any kind of foothold in the conversation flowing around me. I was still thinking about downstairs, to be honest, but it wouldn't have made any odds if I wasn't, because so much of what was said sailed straight over my head. I was surprised, and a bit disappointed, at how narrow people's interests were. There was no hint in their talk of anything Caesar or Claire had said earlier. It was all 'theatre, theatre, theatre,' and lots of names – Peter Brook, Howard Barker, David Hare – that I'd never heard of.

A quarrel broke out, for instance, between Philip and Jim about whether theatre should be considered a spiritual or a political art. Jim was highly animated, as usual, jabbing and pointing like he was the bossman and no-one could argue with him.

'Theatre in its social context is absolutely central, Phil. Caesar understands and appreciates that. A one-size-fits-all mysticism just won't do these days. The hippie era's over. Metaphysics drains the stage of meaning.'

Philip chewed his nails. He took his time, like Claire, in replying, but also like Claire, he spoke well when he did – quiet, a little stuttery, but hypnotic and persuasive. 'C-can the theate ever do anything more, Jim, than add just one single moment to the quality of our awareness and, consequently, to our comprehension of the world and our role and calling in it? The only question, surely, is how to drill down to this rich, fecund level? Which t-tools dig the deepest? The familiar or the unknown? The d-day to day or the mythic? I believe that Caesar understands and appreciates the scale of the challenge that faces us, both on the individual and the corporate level, and I fear that disappointment lies in wait for you, my noble colleague.'

Jim retreated into his soup. He looked cheesed off, for sure – red-faced and rattled – but then Jean-Luc cracked a yarn that perked everyone up.

'In my country,' he began, 'there lives a trickster god named Edshu, who delights in setting snares for the foolish that also enlighten the wise. This same Edshu walked along the path between two fields one morning in a hat that was red on one side, white on the other, green in front and black behind. The locals watched him pass, and, meeting that night in the village square, discussed the odd-looking stranger they had seen.

"A tall man in a red hat," said one.

"Red? Rubbish! It was a black hat."

"No! White."

"What are you all raving about? Are you all blind? His hat was green."

The locals swapped fists, each certain he was right. They were arrested and taken to the cells. Then Edshu showed himself to them in his multi-coloured hat and they fell about laughing. So you see, Philip and James, how truth is capable of wearing more than one hat.'

Everyone laughed, even Jacqueline, who had sat all prim and proper to my right, saying not a word so far. The door opened again. A woman in a black short-sleeved blouse, with mousy brown hair, appeared with a second silver trolley. Everyone, same as before, stood up and walked over. The woman took hold of the first trolley and cleared our tables while we helped ourselves to the main course (cod, beans and broccoli). 'Good evening, Glinka,' said Jim. Glinka smiled, nodded and went quietly on with her business.

I stood in the queue and felt a hand, like an electric shock, on my shoulder. I jumped and turned around. It was Jacqueline. She wore a green, tailored tweed jacket, set off by a bronze, labyrinth-patterned brooch on her left lapel. She stood so tall in front of me, taller even than Vivi, who I'd always considered exceptionally tall. She had a very Roman, slightly crooked nose, which went well, I felt, with her aristocratic manner and bearing. She looked like she'd been to one of those schools where you walk around all day with piles of books on your head. She seemed familiar as well, like I'd seen her before, but couldn't pinpoint quite where. I felt edgy from the start in her presence. I wanted her approval. I wanted to impress. I've no idea why. I've never been like that with anyone else.

'Don't you think,' she said in a cut-glass accent, 'that it's remarkably odd for so many capable, intelligent people to continually refer to Mr. Carlisle as "Caesar?"'

I shrugged and smiled, like a stupid person. Jacqueline carried on. 'It strikes me as perfectly reprehensible. Surely we are all here to learn, not encourage each other in pre-pubescent ego-games."

'I agree,' I babbled (even though I didn't). 'It'd be like me saying everyone should call me "storyteller." Are you an actor too?'

Jacqueline shook her head. 'I'm a historian,' she said. 'Kings.'

'Oh yes, Kings.'

I'd no idea though whether that meant she was a student of the monarchy, or that she'd been to King's College in Cambridge, or even King's Uni in London.

I was dreading having to sit back down and continue the conversation, but Caesar himself came to my rescue, striding into the room from the kitchen door, clad this time in a grey robe with a blue belt, his maroon book in his right hand. Everyone, even Jacqueline, shushed and stood up as he entered. He held his left hand aloft, let it fall, and everyone sat back down. If he was 'peed off' with me and Claire, he didn't show it. Standing in the middle of the room, with no further ado, he opened his book and started to read. I picked up my cutlery, cut the cod and pinned back my ears.

****

'The Saxons were driven back, shattered by Arthur's fury, the Southern and Eastern coasts cleansed of their longships once and for all. The blue-painted Picts meditated war from north of the Wall, but lacked the allies and weapons to back up their threats. The Scots, cut adrift in Hibernia, were unwilling to chance their pirate galleys against the King's swift and powerful ships.

'Arthur's Kingdom, Logres, was secure and established, yet Arthur himself was headstrong and wild, intoxicated by the scale of his success, the valour of his men, the beauty of his wife, Gwenyhffar, and the glory of his capital, Camelot.

"My Lord and King," counselled Merlin one night, as the saffron lamps of the Praetorium swung behind his wild and woolly head. "Do not think now that your service in the cause of right has run its course. On the contrary, it has only just begun. Stasis is the enemy of Logres. Our adversary, the Devil, sleeps not. At the first sign of complacency, he will pounce and work his poison. I urge you, my King, to view these victories as springboards to greater deeds yet, not acts of war this time, but high accomplishments of mind and spirit. When all is weighed and measured, there would be neither point nor purpose to Logres were it to model itself on every other realm on earth – mercantile, self-serving, unimaginative, cold-hearted. Logres must be as a chalice, open always to the Spirit's inspiration. Then, and only then, can it achieve its divine purpose as bearer of the sacred fire, herald of the Golden Age to come – the reign of great Melchizedek, high priest and king – after the consummation of this age."

'So spoke Merlin. I, Taliessin, the King's bard, watching from the antechamber, saw how Arthur threw back his noble, bearded head, laughing loud and long.

"Oh, Merlin, Merlin, wisest and best of counsellors, celebrate our victory, I pray thee. The war is over. Our rage is spent. It has served its purpose. Your high seriousness, my mage, has served its purpose too. So, come with us to the Hall of State. Eat, drink, dance and make merry.'

'Merlin growled and shook his silvery, leonine head from side to side, shrugging off the King's embrace and walking out into the colonnade and the winter air. Arthur stood there for a moment, puzzled and anxious, before the rabble of courtiers and lickspittles cossetted him again with flattery and silky tongues. But I, Taliessin, took note of the matter, stored Merlin's words in my heart and waited for the apposite time.

'That time came soon enough, ten nights on at Lindum. The King ascended the wall to bring bread and hot wine to his men, and when he came down, at the Theodosian Gate, there was I, hiding in the shadows, biding my time.

"My Lord and King."

"Taliessin, my princely bard." He slapped me across the shoulders. He was young still, and the wine (which had clearly been shared with his men) had clearly gone to his head.

We walked towards the Praetorium. A thin wind blew.

"My Liege. You will forgive me, I hope. The eyes and ears of a bard are everywhere. They need to be. Otherwise, our reservoir of songs and stories will run dry. It is ten days and nights, is it not, since the Lord Merlin spoke with you?"

"Ah, Merlin," the King laughed. "He has retired to the woods, sulking like the Saxons, because we refused to give ground to his strategy of never-ending spiritual war."

'I then performed a risky, though finely-calibrated action, grasping my Sovereign by his shoulders and pulling him towards me, into the fiery glow of the sentry-house brazier.

"My Lord and King. The wise, noble Merlin is right. I urge you, with all the loyalty I owe and all the love I bear, to act on his advice. The Devil sleeps not. That, at least, is true. And Merlin – part-god, part-man, part-beast – perceives and understands so much more than we do. Everything, thus far, that he has prophecied, has come true. Greater things yet has he prophecied. I pray you, with all the respect my vocation commands, to go in pilgrimage to the Rialto Cathedral and stand before the Oval Mirror, that sacred skin of glass that shows the secrets of what was, what is, and is to come."

"Past, present and future, in other words," snorted the King. "What good are these three imposters? The past is gone; the future, as you say, yet to come; and the present ruled and mastered by our royal person."

'I retracted not my words. Arthur turned and stalked away, but I was certain, by the set of his gait that he would do as I suggested. He could not ignore both his mage and his bard. Ten nights on, by the statue of Constantine at York, he told me what transpired.'

****

I nearly choked on a piece of fish. The 'Rialto Cathedral' was my own creation, you see, taken from the *Macbeth* essay Mr. Martin had sent Caesar. From now on in, swap Macbeth for Arthur, and Scotland for Logres, and a couple of other bits and bobs, and it was my story entirely...

****

'The King rode South West that night, to the point where Logres, the sea, and the dream-laden realm of Broceliande meet. The Rialto

Cathedral, with its green, luminous dome, stood high on the rocks, overlooking the sea. Arthur was met there by monks and nuns in robes of blue and white. They fed and tethered his horse, then warmed the King with soup and broth, before he went his way, walking alone into the High Place.

'He stood before the Mirror in the Nave of a Thousand Candles. At first he saw nothing, save the Mirror's bottle-green surface and the candles' quivering, glimmering reflection. He began to believe that nothing further would occur; that the Oval Mirror was a mere old wives tale, nothing more. But then came a face, rising to the top, flickering and unsteady at first, followed by the figure of a crowned, bejewelled king on a throne. This king was young and angry, his mouth a bellowing tunnel, his blazing eyes as red as blood. Everything about him was red – countenance, costume, crown, eyes, jewellery, shield and sword. He roared and shouted, with implacable urgency, but the King of Logres heard not a word.

'The vision sunk and subsided into depths of mysterious, glassy waters. Once again, Arthur beheld the Mirror's mingled, rippling screen of green and gold. Then, after a time, the waves settled and ceased, and an older sovereign appeared, seated on an ornate throne, with a silver crown and garments of purple, white and blue. He bore in his right hand a scpetre, and in his left an orb. Behind his head were mountains, and men and women – pecked incessantly by sombre black birds – passing between and along the mountains on pack horses and mules. The king's eyes shifted, up and down uneasily, like he wished to watch the migrations behind him, but remained unable, either through enchantment or infirmity of spirit, to turn, see and act.

'A black-winged bird flew across the Mirror, from left to right, and the King of the Mountains vanished. Once more only candles and bottle-green ripples met the King's anxious, puzzled gaze. Then, for no reason at all, the air around him lightened. Vitality and freshness – inexplicably, unaccountably – surged through his body, mind and spirit, like spring rain or summer lightning. The Mirror, for the third time, changed tone and texture – ripples becoming waves, waves becoming a bay – and on that bay – under a sky of blue – ringed by white, jagged rocks – sat a girl up on top with a green headscarf and blue mantle blowing in the wind. In her hands she held a harp.

'The nave grew warmer, the flames leapt and swayed, as first her music, then her song, penetrated the King's heart, until he fell on his knees on the stone and wept and wept and wept as he had not done since his favourite hound, Cabal, had died when he was a boy.

'Gradually the loss and sorrow left him, and he was quiet and still in his soul, as he had never been in his life before – not in war, nor peace, nor camaraderie, nor even friendship and love. The purity of the song and the music's wild, untameable beauty called to something deeper, richer and higher in him – a sphere of silence and grace – a region of mystery and unforeseen, unsuspected possibilities that – he told me in York – felt somehow familiar and strange, joyous and sad, victorious and elegiac, all at the same time. It was the type of song, he said, that could only be heard at the end of the world – by which he meant, I believe, not only the coming consummation of this age, but also the Westernmost extremity of Earth itself, that point at the rim of the horizon, where stars meet water meet sky, where this world meets the next, and where our Sovereign Lady, Bridget of the Starry Eyes, goddess of music and stories, keeper of dreams and prophecies, keeps her seat and sings her song atop the white, jagged rocks.'

XIII

I had a powerful dream, later that night, where all of us at the table were sat in a circle again, but this time under the stars, around a crackling, roaring bonfire. We all wore coloured tunics. Mine was green with a silver circle. Jacqueline was sat cross-legged to my right. Hers was white with a purple diamond.

A man stood by the fire, in the centre of the circle, reading aloud from a book. It was a story or myth of some kind, which in my dream I found totally captivating, but when I woke up could remember nothing about at all. The man was clad in gold. That was what I recalled. His hair was as white as Jacqueline's tunic. It wasn't Ambrosius Carlisle. Or anyone else. No. It was my dad.

Sunbeams, when I awoke, slanted through the curtains and onto the floor, bathing the room in a sub-aquatic sheen, that, for the second time in under twenty four hours, made me think of Blue Planet. I kicked off the sheets and sprang into life.

Looking back now, I think I expected every day at Constantine's Chambers to be as full-on and intense as the first. It didn't pan out like that – well, not until last night – but I never felt disappointed or let down. Quite the reverse. There was no sense of rush or haste, you see. That was the thing. I remember bounding down the stairs that first morning, pumped up for drama and action, but it was stillness, calm and peace that met me instead – panelled, book-lined rooms; long silent corridors; soft lamplight at night; and shaded bay windows to sit, dream and think in during the day, as yellowgold leaves leapt, spun, twisted and swirled in the autumn sun outside.

It's totally astonishing – a complete and utter mystery – how everything went to pot so quickly. The whole set-up seemed so stable and solid. Slow as well. All of October, plus the first half of November, felt so much longer than a mere month and a half. Time dragged at Constantine's Chambers. But not in a bad way. Not at all. The easy pace settled me down and helped me dig deeper, both into myself and, once I'd been told what it was, into the story Caesar had brought me there to write.

I thought a lot about Gina, now at Leeds Uni, and jammy Anna Charpentier, down at The Courtauld, and the very different life they'd have been living – the hoo-hah of 'Welcome Week', loads of new people to meet, so many things to do, the buzz of a new city, and so forth. Life at Constantine's Chambers, I reckoned, was pretty much at the 'antipodes', as Dr. Tenby sometimes said, of all that.

Claire, I should say, was spot on in what she'd told me. We had indeed been given a 'watching brief', and that seemed to suit us both fine.

She'd spend ages each day in the studio, and I'd go there often as well, just to sit and watch, or lie on the floor sometimes, close my eyes and chill. I never said anything, and neither did Claire, but I had the sense that she liked me being there. She told me once, in Marie Louise Gardens (a five minute walk from Constantine's Chambers – go there sometime, they're beautiful) that she sometimes got very 'het up' and angry when painting – shouting and swearing and flinging her arms about. But I saw nothing of that. She was always a model of serenity to me.

We grew close. We'd often walk down by the river together (the Mersey itself, believe it or not, though totally titchy compared to how it is in Liverpool), through the Botanical Gardens and around the leafy Didsbury backstreets. I liked South Manchester in many ways, though I didn't, on the whole, go out all that much on my own, apart from the occasional bus ride up to the Holy Name Church on Oxford Road.

Didsbury 'Village', as everyone calls it, boasts a lot of cafés and bars, and one or two Constantine's Chambers types (including myself, as you'll hear in a bit) had part-time jobs there. I found it a bit posh at times (too many 'yummy mummies' for my liking) but generally speaking it was okay. Now and again we'd pop out for a coffee or drink, either to 'Expo Lounge', where Claire worked, or the 'Art of Tea,' which has a boss second-hand bookshop attached to the back.

My relations with everyone else in the house (apart from Jacqueline) never really got going. Jean-Luc, Camilla, Philip and Jim spent most of their days working with Caesar on *Macbeth*. They rehearsed in the 'Drama Space', a first floor room directly above the art studio and exactly the same shape and size. Now and then they disappeared down the dining room stairs to the mysterious 'stage-set' – always with Caesar, the sheepdog, behind them – but I never asked anyone what they did, or saw, or if there was a chapel or anything like that. I had a strong feeling though – stronger every day – that the 'cubby-hole' door had been left unlocked on purpose that first afternoon, for someone – most likely myself – to find it, walk down and see what I saw. I tried not to dwell on it. I didn't want to big myself up or think I was special or 'chosen' in any way. It was hard though. It all tied in so incredibly well, both with the stories Dad had told me and the ones I'd created myself. I found myself wondering too, daft though it sounds, if the door had been hidden from my sight that first day by some kind of 'magic mist', like the wizards and priests used to conjure up in the stories, making both people and things invisible.

Technically, Claire and I were allowed, and even encouraged as part of our 'watching brief', to attend rehearsals, but Claire never went at all (she was always too busy) and I only sat in once. The first thing I noted (this was in the Drama Space) was that all four actors were dressed in coloured tunics, just like the ones in my wardrobe.

This wearing of tunics, I should say, was one of the rules of the house. Whenever engaged in creative work, Caesar instructed us, we were always to don a tunic. It didn't matter which one – we could take our pick – just as long as we had one on. 'It will bring an extra, mythically-charged dimension to your work,' he said. Caesar himself never wore a tunic though. He always wore a robe – usually black, blue, white or grey – with a matching felt hat and a rope-belt of contrasting colour.

Caesar did all the talking, the time I was there. The others sat around him in a semi-circle on the stage, while I leant against a pillar at the far end of the room. Caesar had his back to me.

'The chief consideration,' he said, 'when playing Shakespeare, is not to lose yourself in *sturm und drang* concerning your character but to focus on the poetry and music. It is by music, word music, that Shakespeare expresses his vision, and if you connect with the music, the character will take shape, and you will drill down to those latent depths and powers within, which Constantine's Chambers exists to bring to the surface.

'To illustrate, let me present, if I may, an example from my own career. I was playing Richard III in Tariq Vintner's production at the Almeida in 1992. Now, Tariq had given me a colossal iron weapon, like a mace, with a ball and spikes at each end, to brandish in the battle scene. I complained like billy-o. I told him it was too heavy. Far too heavy. I could hardly pick the damn thing up, let alone carry it and cast it back and forth as a weapon.' (Everyone laughed at this point. Jim, I noticed, had a very toothy grin). 'I was frustrated. I wanted the production to be like this one – no props, no accoutrements – but in the end I didn't have a choice and was compelled to cede the point, flying down a flight of steps with the infernal object in my hands, crying:

Let us to't pell-mell. If not to Heaven, then hand in hand to Hell.

'While running I lifted, then wielded the weapon above my head, swinging it around with considerable difficulty, like a battle axe. But then, my students, just as I began to shout – yes, precisely at that moment – the breakthrough came. My spirit, oppressed no longer by the weapon's weight, but liberated by Shakespeare's poetry, soared above and beyond the confines of the stage and the limitations of my earthly frame. The mace, as my lines erupted – exploded, even – from the depths of my being, carried no weight at all. A baby could have held it. The matchless poetry, the drama, intensity and sheer bloody madness of it all, had either dissolved it to nothing or I had become, under this most *puissant* of influences, a thousand times more potent. Such, my students, is the royal, transformative power to be mined and tapped within, nurtured, then transposed from Shakespeare's stage to the currently empty stage of contemporary politics, culture and society.'

I chose that moment to slip away. I never went to the Drama Space again. Not because I didn't want to or hadn't buzzed off what Caesar was saying (Christ, no) but because I felt I didn't really belong there and that he wasn't talking to me but the actors, and that when he did talk to me he'd have something different to say, something meant only for me.

It wouldn't have mattered anyway. The actors were a quiet, thoughtful bunch and tended to keep themselves to themselves. Even Jim, once rehearsals started, cut out the banter and got his head down. It was a strange business. People I'd expected to play big roles in my time at Constantine's Chambers were now, all of a sudden, acting out bit-parts at best, like extras or props – 'accoutrements' even.

Jacqueline Cutter, of course, is anything but a bit-part figure in this story, but she too played a low-key role at that time. I used to see her more than anyone else at dinner (I never bothered with breakfast, and there wasn't a lunch), which, I should say, was always – after my first night – served at half-seven on the dot in the dining room. It was a warm buffet basically: curry one night, fish the next, pizza the evening after, and so on, always with a nice bowl of soup and a chunk of bread first up to get us going. Lolek and Glinka did the honours, and it was always dead tasty, though sometimes there was hardly anyone there due to work commitments and what not. Caesar never read aloud again either, though he ate with us most Sundays and told us tales from his life, usually ending up by praising drama and literature as 'fountains of vitality' and dissing academia as 'Satan's sterile Kingdom.'

'You will all know what I mean by that,' he commented one evening, 'having passed through the cobwebbed rooms of our theory-infected, godless, so-called Higher Education Institutions.' He glanced across at me and smiled. 'All except Miss Carlton, of course, Liverpool's own Taliessin. Ah, how lucky you are, Miss Carlton, and how also how wise, to choose this side of the river rather than that.' I felt myself blush. Everyone was gawping. I felt dead embarrassed. I made eye contact with Claire, and she winked, which was nice. Then Lolek came to take the plates. He ruffled my hair as he passed and I was sound as a pound again.

Lolek always had that effect on me. I hit it off with Glinka and him right from the start. They looked after the cleaning as well, you see, and sometimes I'd offer to lend a hand with a bit of sweeping or dusting. I'm not sure, to be honest, that anyone else did, even Claire, and I think they liked me for that. It helped that I knew a few Polish words as well, picked up from Adam and Cecylia, our lodgers back in the day at Canning Street. It was simple stuff – 'thank you': *dziękuję*, 'you're welcome': *nie ma za co* – but I could tell they appreciated the effort. 'We will have you reading Sienkiewicz in no time, Miss Julie,' Lolek said one mizzly morning over a ciggie out the back (Lolek, Glinka and I were the only smokers) as he pretended to thwack me around the chops with a feather duster.

Anyway, back to Jacqueline. As I said before, I found her frightfully upper class, and there was something forbidding and austere in her manner that made me all jittery and tongue-tied in her presence. Despite this, I could tell deep down that she was basically friendly and sincere, or was at least trying to be. Whenever Claire wasn't about (which was a lot, as Claire was the hardest working of us all, both paid and unpaid) she'd sit beside me at dinner and ask about my favourite books, paintings, films, etc. But when I'd ask similar things, she'd 'clam up' all of a sudden. 'Oh, you know,' she'd say. 'I'm just a dry as dust historian.' Claire reckoned she was writing an essay on the Enlightenment – some kind of defence of Enlightenment values – due to be published in next year's *Chlorian Review*. She'd been given a special bursary from the EU apparently, just for this work, which meant she couldn't get involved in any of our theatrical, artistic or storytelling activities.

She was a funny one, for sure, but I didn't hear her criticise Caesar again, not to my face anyway, and not for a long time. I knew what she meant in some ways. I mean, it certainly seemed silly for a fella of forty (maybe fifty) odd to insist on everyone calling him 'Caesar'. But come on, really, what of it? That's just the way his imagination works. It's what turns him on, gets him going and makes him such a top notch teacher and performer – just ask the school groups that come, spellbound by his sensational one man show, where, for one blistering hour, he's Richard II, Richard III, Hamlet, Macbeth, Lear and Prospero, one after the other, in a virtuoso display of everything drama should be. And that was why we were there, surely. To learn, as Jacqueline herself had put it. 'Pre-pubescent ego games' or whatever it was didn't come into it. We'd gone to Constantine's Chambers to learn from a true M.A – a Master of Arts. I failed to see why a bloke like that was expected to be so totally straight and normal, like he was a banker or an 'economic forecaster' or something equally humdrum.

This became one of my beefs with Romulus Charles as well.

Romulus Charles.

Even the sound of that silly name in my head sets my teeth on edge. I'm going to find this part of my story acutely embarrassing, but time's cracking on, there might not be much of it left, so I've got to tell it, and it goes like this:

Just as Claire seemed to spend half her life in the studio and half at Expo, Jacqueline divided her time, it appeared, between the Constantine's Chambers library and the 'Sevastopol Suite', a pseudo-East European coffee shop and bar on Crossway, one of the side-streets off Barlow Moor Road, where, by co-incidence, I'd got myself a bit of work – just two shifts to keep me in clover – Wednesdays ten till six and Fridays five till one.

I took a bit of a shine, God alone knows why, to the café owner, Romulus Charles. It seems so stupid now, given everything that's happened and remembering what a dicksplat he was (and is if he survived last night), but there you go. I can't deny it, and can't pretend it didn't happen. Much as I'd like to.

'Rommie,' as he styled himself, must have been about thirty or so, miles older than either Jacqueline (who's twenty-six) or myself. His face was chiselled; his eyes a slithery, shifting blue. His hair was already grey, which gave him a striking, distinctive look. He was slim and well-toned, and came from down south somewhere, though I never found out exactly where. His accent was more drawly than Claire's, but not as posh as Jacqueline's or Caesar's. He had tattoos on his arms, wore well-fitted t-shirts, and said he was a novelist and that his heroes were Ian McEwan and Julian Barnes. This really excited me. I'd never read either of those authors, but I was all a-flutter that he was into books. I poured everything out. I told him about Rosemary Sutcliff – *The Lantern Bearers* and all that – and he snorted with derision in reply. I was crushed. Stamped on and destroyed. 'It would be comical if it wasn't so tragic, Julie,' he told me, wiping down the counter with a 'designer' Soviet-flag-style rag. 'I mean, this regression to personal and political infancy your guru continually advocates.'

The name, Ambrosius Carlisle, as you can tell, cut no ice at all. 'I'm not sure we've room for such anachronistic thinking, certainly not such dubious political views, in today's Didsbury,' was all he said, before changing the subject to the previous night's takings being twenty quid down.

I should have left. I really should. I did in the end, of course, but I should have quit sooner. Much sooner. Romulus Charles didn't rate me. That was the top and bottom of it. He saw me as a child. Didn't take me seriously. He only took me on because I'd worked at FACT and knew what I was doing making coffee. As I say, it pissed me off, and disturbed the peace and calm I had come to know and love at Constantine's Chambers. It made me realise how much, over the years, I'd actually been totally spoilt and had got used to people of substance making a fuss of me, being bothered where my head was at, and taking my artistic and spiritual views seriously. I mattered. They cared: Dad, Vivi, Mr. Martin, Dr. Tenby, Caesar definitely, even Jacqueline in her own way.

Jacqueline! Now there's the rub. There was one person 'Rommie' Charles had bags of time for. She was there so much, and so often I'd see them together, talking and laughing, either at the bar or one of the little round tables. Jacqueline was totally different in the Sevastopol Suite, hair down, long and brown, and glasses gone. Her eyes twinkled. She smiled more than I'd ever seen her smile at CC. Her face was a revelation – lively, playful and relaxed.

Romulus Charles looked very much at home in her company as well. He'd make a lot of open, positive gestures with his hands while he was talking to her, and then, when she was talking to him, he'd smile, not with his lips but with his eyes, if that makes sense. I'd have given anything to be part of their conversation. I really would. But I never got the chance. They never let me near. Jacqueline was friendly enough, but not in the way she was at CC. Her eyes weren't twinkling for me. That was for sure. I felt excluded – locked out – ordered to keep my distance through not so subtle hints of body language. 'Over there, I'm a writer,' I thought. 'Here, just a waiter.' It bugged the Hell out of me, if I'm honest.

Not that I saw them touching or kissing or anything. They weren't 'going out' with each other. No way. They were hardly ever alone in any case. There were always a fair few punters, I noticed, milling around wherever Jacqueline was: hipsters with big beards, glamourous looking women – actress/model types – and even some hard-looking cases, boxers or gangsters, perhaps. I never saw her especially 'close' with any of them, but I was fascinated, I confess, with what wheels might be turning behind that studious 'defence of Enlightenment values' exterior. Because something was afoot. Clearly.

One night, the mask nearly slipped. Jacqueline and Romulus, together with a few randoms, were sat in the 'Fall of the Wall Room' under the Gorbachev poster. I swung by, picked up the empties, heard the words 'citizen's arrest' (from Jacqueline, I think), then saw both of them shoot me a glare, which basically said I shouldn't have been there and shouldn't have heard what I'd just heard. Jacqueline put her hand to her mouth. Her face turned the colour of boiled shite. But I was tired. It had been a busy night. I couldn't be bothered with it. Much as I wanted to be part of their scene, I couldn't be doing with what was odds-on some kind of post-modern (a favourite Romulus phrase) word game, which would wind up with me looking daft in front of them both. No thanks!

Anyway, I was feeling less wound up than usual that night. I'd had bigger fish to fry that day, you see, Friday November 14th. Because that was the day Caesar invited me back to his chamber to officially give me my assignment (or 'mission', as he called it).

So, there I was, perched on the sofa again, with Caesar sat on the throne-like chair this time. Music drifted up from the kitchen – the '80s station Lolek liked that actually, now I think of it, gave me the only music I ever heard at Constantine's Chambers. I'm not one for IPods and headphones, I should say. I like to hear the world around me, both when I'm out and about and when I'm on my own. It helps me think. Helps me dig down. Helps me connect and create.

I knew all the tunes inside out. Dad used to have them on in the house when we were little: *Gold, Betty Davis Eyes, Flashdance* (I used to dance around the room to that), *We Built This City*, and so on. Caesar, perhaps surprisingly, seemed to enjoy the music too. He must have done, I suppose, otherwise he wouldn't have let Lolek have it on. He had that boyish, impish look again. I thought he might pull out the globe and test my catching again, but he spoke instead, and seriously too. It was a strange conversation to have with *Billie Jean* in the background.

'Tell me *Mith* Carlton, please, would you consider yourself a churchgoer in any way?'

'K-kind of, Sir. Caesar, I mean. I get the bus to the Uni sometimes and sit in the big church there. The Holy Name. But only when it's quiet and there's no-one there. I like the stillness and the silence.'

'Very wise, very wise. You don't hear Mass then?'

'Not really. That's more my sister's thing. I find Mass quite hard, to be honest, Caesar. Too much chatter and noise. Not enough quiet.'

'You believe in God though?'

'Yes.'

'What kind of God?'

'A goddess, Caesar.'

'What kind of goddess then?'

'The missing goddess.'

'Missing? Why?'

'She sang to me twice. I missed her song. Both times.'

'How?'

'First time I saw something in a window and got distracted; second time the vision faded.'

'Visions often do.'

'It's stayed with me though.'

'I know. That's why you're here.'

He stroked his beard. He looked like a Russian priest.

'She comes to me often though,' I continued, warming to my theme, like I was back in Room B6 with Mr. Martin. 'Through stories and myths, I mean – my father's, my own – the legends and tales of the West. I used to believe I'd never hear or see her again – physically, I mean – but now I'm beginning to think that I might. Maybe at the end of time. The c-consummation of the age. I try not to think that I'm special, but maybe I am. Maybe that's my vocation. Maybe *that's* why I'm here.'

Robert de Niro's Waiting by Bananarama started up downstairs. Caesar smiled, like he knew what I was playing at, stood up, turned around, walked to the window, and refused to take the bait. When he replied, his back to me still, it was like he was Chief Prosecutor or something, summing me up in a court of law. 'Most interesting. Most interesting. You have a relationship with Divinity, that is clear. An unusual, highly individual relationship, but a relationship nonetheless, and a strong one at that.'

I don't need a boy, I got a man of steel...

I squidged up to the right on the sofa a bit and was got a slight view of the spire, which was nice. Sun glinted on its lightbrick facade. Leaves tumbled. Caesar turned around and looked me in the eye.

'And this relationship is of the absolute essence. It is the one thing needed.' He took his chair and sat back down. 'The tide, Miss Carlton, rushes in upon us. Liberalism, materialism and individualism have ravaged the West from within, and our civilisation stands ripe for conquest, assaulted by aggressive secularism on one side and radical Islam on the other. Nature abhors a vacuum, and that, I am afraid, is where we are living – in a spiritual, cultural and political vacuum. It will be filled, one way or the other. Conquest, as I say, approaches – a world of discipline without liberty, or – perhaps worse – a world shorn of all discipline. A world where the human person is either fully subsumed to the collective, or where the very concepts of personhood and society are lost in a morass of decadent individualism. The only hope we have – our community's *raison d'être* – is to rediscover some spiritual flair and reconstruct that two-way street between the human and the ancient, eternal light, that the Hebrew prophets – Elijah, Daniel, *et al* – as much as the Greek and Roman sages dedicated their lives to.'

He opened out his hands to me, as if it was *him* that needed *me*, as if it was *me* doing *him* a favour, not him giving me the chance of a lifetime. '*Thith* is why, Miss Carlton, I would like your story to take as it's starting point the Second World War and a hypothetical British defeat at the Battle of Britain. I would like you to meditate on how and why, where and when, in what shape and form, an Arthurian-style Resistance might have emerged. I know that your interests include Shakespeare and mythology, alongside wartime and post-Roman Britain, and this is where your teacher, David Martin, and myself, believe your writing has its unique edge. You can use Miss Falconer's art as inspiration if you wish, but please do not feel that your mission has to contain itself within a commentary on her paintings. I want what only you, Miss Carlton, out of all our noble colleagues, can bring to our table – vision and creative fire – an individual, imaginative, dynamic response – a story, a myth, a fresh angle – not a sermon, thesis, or list of facts.'

What a speech. I felt on fire. He stood up. I thought he was done. He took off his hat and threw it me. I caught it, held it, stroked it. Ceasar carried on.

'Trust your horse, my child. Let your imagination guide you to the treasure at the centre of the labyrinth. The acting group and I, alchemists that we are, will mould and shape, transmute and transform, your raw creative spark. Take then, as you go, as prayer and benediction, these words of Theseus in *A Midsummer Night's Dream*:

The poet's eye, in a fine frenzy rolling,
Doth glance from Heaven to earth, from earth to Heaven;
And, as imagination bodies forth
The forms of things unknown, the poet's pen
Turns them to shapes, and gives to airy nothing
A local habitation and a name.

'I have been aware of your latent potential for a long time, Miss Carlton. This assignment, I know, chimes and resonates with what and who you are, just as it represents the spiritual, philosophical core of Constantine's Chambers. In the words of Blake:

I give you the end of a golden string,

Only wind it into a ball,

It will lead you in at Heaven's gate

Built in Jerusalem's wall.'

Goodness me! What could I say? What could I do? When could I start? I was desperate to crack straight on, but I had to be at the silly Sevastopol Suite for a quarter to five and it was already gone four. It was so busy that night that it knocked the stuffing out of me a bit, and I didn't feel like writing the next day, even though I was sure I would, or the next day either, or the day after that.

I spent the whole week, as much of it as I could, in my room in the end, just reading and reflecting – 'meditating', as Caesar had said. On the Saturday – November 22nd – I went down to the library after lunch, hoping I could find something extra to give me a spark.

I liked the library a lot. It reminded me of the St. Mark's library, with its high shelves, tiled floor, old-school tables and chairs and art-deco reading lamps. Someone had left a book on one of the orange tasselled rugs. I bent down and grabbed it, instinctively. It was an exhibition catalogue:

Stations of the Cross by Rob Floyd, Manchester Cathedral, Lent and Easter 2014.

I flicked through the book, took it with me to the nearest desk, and realised there and then, right on the spot, that I'd got it – my story, myth and angle. Out it came, fully formed, like Athene springing from the head of Zeus. All I needed was a name for my hero. I put the book down and ran out of the library, up the stairs to my room. On the way I cracked it.

'Take two teachers,' I said to myself, 'any two, say, Dr. Tenby and Miss DuVal. Good. Now, take his first name and her last name, and there we are – Ronald DuVal. No, that's bit dull. How about Ronnie DuVal? Yes, that's better, that's it – Ronnie DuVal.'

I ripped off my red dress and everything else and left them all in a pile at the foot of the bed. I opened the wardrobe, took out and stepped into the pale blue tunic with the orange ball of fire. It was my first time in a tunic, and I didn't feel silly or daft at all. It felt good. Like I'd come home. I tied it with the red belt, slipped into my silver-buckled shoes, then took down my copy of *Ulysses*. There was a paragraph in it I liked that would do as an epigraph.

I raced back down the stairs. By the time I reached the door I had my hero pictured in my mind, who else but the man in the pink shirt and blue serge jacket, with the grey shaggy mane, streaked with black and white, who'd smiled at me the evening I drank from Vivi's chalice.

By the time I got to the desk, I had my title. There could only be one. There only ever was one ...

XIV

Saint Mark's

The gods too are ever kind, Lenehan said. If I had poor luck with Bass's mare perhaps this draught of his may serve me more propensely. He was laying his hands upon a winejar; Malachi saw it and withheld his act, pointing to the stranger and to the scarlet label. Warily, Malachi whispered, preserve a druid silence. His soul is far away. It is as painful perhaps to be awakened from a vision as to be born. Any object, intensely regarded, may be a gate of access to the incorruptible aeon of the gods.

James Joyce, *Ulysses*.

'Julie.'

I'm not sure how many times he called my name. I didn't even know he was standing beside me. The college library, wrapped around in rain and cloud, always sweeps me off on wet, mizzly days to mist-shrouded realms of myth and magic. It was gone half-three, and there was only me in the library.

'Julie.'

My finger was still on the page. The story I had been reading – Theseus and the Minotaur – rang on and on like a gong in my mind.

'Julie.'

I turned around. Mr. Martin, my English teacher, was standing to my left in his blue, roll-neck sweater. His black hair and beard, so Gina reckons (she's my best friend), makes him look like Captain Haddock in the Tintin books. He pulled up a chair and coughed. Rat-tat-tat went the rain on the windows. 'Sister Mary Margaret,' he began, 'has asked if you could pop across to Manchester, Julie, and have a look at Ronnie DuVal's *Stations of the Cross* in the Cathedral. She'd like you to write a piece for *The Winged Lion*.' (That's our college magazine, by the way).

I couldn't make head nor tail of what he was saying. I felt all flustered and confused. 'A piece, Sir? Manchester, Sir?'

Mr. Martin's voice was kind and patient. 'Sister believes,' he explained, 'that St. Mark's should learn to stretch its wings, as it were, and engage a little more with events of interest outside Merseyside.'

I shook my head, stretching out my fingers on the table's ancient wood. 'I don't know, Sir. I'm not really into Art, Sir. I like the piccies in storybooks, but that's about it.' I pointed to the book and the drawing of Theseus following the golden thread – around and around, this way and that – back and forth through the depths of the labyrinth. 'It's words I'm interested in, Sir. You know that. It's sound of Sister to ask and I'm dead grateful, I really am, but someone like Anna Charpentier'd be miles better, if you want my opinion, Sir. She's mad about art. She's applying to The Courtauld for next year, you know.'

Mr. Martin fixed his sea-green eyes on me. He stood up and scraped back his chair on the chequerboard floor.

'Stop babbling, Julie. It's you that Sister wants and that's that. She knows what you're about. Society needs a shot of what you've got, she says – vision and fire. That's what she wants from you – an imaginative, dynamic response – a story, a myth, a fresh angle – not a sermon or a thesis on art.' He walked to the door. 'Remember William Blake,' he called out over his shoulder. 'Remember that quote I gave you last week.'

Then he was gone. I puffed out my cheeks and glanced down again at Theseus tip-toeing his way through the labyrinth's weaving, winding corridors.

My 'away day' took place on the last Thursday before the Easter holidays. The sky in Liverpool was a mix of sun and white streaky cloud. In Manchester it was all cloud – heavy and dull. I got lost for a bit, walking from Oxford Road to the Cathedral. The city felt all on top of me – hard-edged and cold – trapping me – hemming me – wedging me in between high bullying buildings and pile after pile of brutalistic steel and glass.

It took me a while, once inside the Cathedral, to find my bearings. The walls shimmered and swam before my eyes, but the old-world smell of the columns and stones settled me down and slowed the whirling in my head. It made me think of the lush, panelled bookshelves lining the long, silent corridors in the St. Mark's library.

The floor was marble and shiny. Tall windows, to my left, glittered with red and yellow interlocking squares and circles.

Candles flickered, to my right, on either side of a white, stone altar. The paintings – Ronnie DuVal's *Stations of the Cross* – surrounded me, pinned to thick, dark pillars that curved up and joined together at the top. The air was cool; the atmosphere calm and still. I weaved my way around, in and out of the pillars, and let the pictures tell their story.

I was moved, more than anything else, by the agony stamped on Jesus' face throughout – his frightened eyes, his bared teeth, his screaming mouth. When he meets his mother it made me want to cry – the way she gazes up at him with such strong love – a love full of sorrow and pain but passing somehow beyond them as well – a love so rich and deep it could walk through walls.

I found the one where Jesus is nailed to the cross incredibly, painfully powerful. The old man hammering in the nail must, I felt sure, be able to hear his screams, but he pays no attention and just carries on banging. Not in a nasty, vicious way though. There's a softness and tenderness to his face that's just so beautiful. He made me think of Dad. I don't know why.

Some of the paintings scared me. Jesus looks frightened out of his mind in the one where he's fallen down with horses hooves and people's feet kicking around above him. His eyes are gone. He's lost and helpless. A baby again. Then when he dies – in black and white – it's like the whole world's abandoned and forgotten him, apart from that big cheesy moon in the top left corner.

The pictures aren't all sad though. I love the colour and dazzle of the Women of Jerusalem and how they just stand there, brassy as anything, and look you right in the eye. When Christ is stripped of his clothes as well, there's a bright white light that quivers around his head. One of the blokes crucified with him sees it. The other doesn't.

There's light everywhere in the paintings. They overflow with light. Two images towards the end stand out for me like this: the one where everyone gathers around the tomb, and the one when the angels appear to say that he's risen. There's a warm, joyful glow in both, full of hope and goodness, but at the same time a bit remote and out of reach, not yet a proper part of our daily lives. Not at the minute anyway. I couldn't remember Mr. Martin's Blake quote, but I did recall another line he gave us one time, from a German poet whose name I can never remember: 'Life in this world is no dream,' said the poet. 'But it could and should become one.'

I sat on top of a rough-hewn slab, swinging my legs forward and back against the stone. I thought about my life and all the question marks hovering around it. Should I really go to Constantine's Chambers? Wouldn't I be better at Uni, after all? Maybe I should stay at home? Or go and live with my sister in London?

What about Ma? Would it he right to leave her? She already thinks that Vivi's deserted her. How do I talk to her about her boozing and what have you?

Then there's my own stuff. Should I carry on with these stories? Aren't I getting a bit old for these myths and legends? Shouldn't I get a bit more experience here and there? Why do I write anyway? Where does it come from? Who is it for? Myself? God? Dad? Mr. Martin? Vivi?

Who am I? Why am I here? And now that I *am* here, what am I meant to do? What's my calling? My vocation? My role?

I focused my eyes on the light, the angels in the cave, Mary Magdalene (I think) listening to their message, and the pale fire trembling in the middle – a jet of quivering white and blue – flaring up from the centre of the earth. I scrunched up my eyes and concentrated as hard as I could, as if some secret or code that could answer my questions might be hidden there, embedded in the texture and lines of the canvas.

A window at the far end of the Cathedral, a stained-glass ball of fire, caught my eye – a swirling, billowing, raging bull of red and orange flame. It looked like the picture-book Dad showed me before he died – *Liverpool at War* – and the photos of burning, blazing warehouses at Herculaneum Dock.

I spotted (so I thought) a faint lined pattern superimposed on the flames, a tissue of wafer-thin diamonds that merged together to form a picture. I honestly thought, crazy though it sounds, that a winged lion started slowly taking shape on the sizzling glass. I jumped down from the slab, inched forward and stood up on tip-toes to get a better look.

'Julie.'

I turned around and swear I saw a figure there above the slab, an angel in maroon and silver, with a flaming sword in one hand and a bronze spear with a blood-red tip in the other. I bowed my head, looked up again, and he (or she) was gone. 'I imagined it,' I said to myself. 'I'm always imagining things.'

Then I realised that it didn't matter. It made no odds. I had my fresh angle. My story. My myth ...

*

... Ronnie DuVal was an artist who lived and worked in Manchester before the Second World War. In 1939 he joined the army as a captain in the Tank Corps. But when, one year later, the Battle of Britain was lost, Parliament surrendered straightaway, so Captain DuVal saw no action in the conflict.

After the Treaty of Cambridge, the Germans occupied the whole of Southern England and the Midlands, leaving Wales, Scotland and the North in British hands, but run by a puppet government based in ex-factory premises in Manchester City Centre.

Disgusted, Ronnie DuVal left the city with his wife, parents and young child. He bought an Edwardian mansion in Liverpool called Saint Mark's, a former monastery, and slowly but steadily began to build up an artistic and philosophical community there. He believed that British society had lost its way before the war and that the country would never again be free until it rediscovered what he called its 'spiritual flair' – its 'vision and creative fire.' He argued that genuine, far-reaching change could only occur through a 'two-way street' between the human and the divine. He spoke often of Elijah, Daniel, and the other Old Testament prophets, and he loved to quote Blake's verse:

I give you the end of a golden string

Only wind it into a ball,

It will lead you in at Heaven's gate

Built in Jerusalem's wall.

One day, Captain DuVal built a labyrinth with his son, Constantine, out of the bookshelves in the college library. He placed one of his famous 1934 *Stations of the Cross* – 'The Angels' – in the centre.

That same afternoon, a girl from Canning Street, Liverpool 8, arrived at St. Mark's, in search of hope, adventure, and answers to her questions. Her name was Geraldine.

It was raining when she reached the blue and gold double doors. A small winged lion, engraved in silver on the wood, appeared, for a moment, to wink at her. Geraldine pushed the door open, and the first thing she saw was a chair to her right with a ball of golden string on the white, upholstered seat ...

*

Julie Caroline Carlton

Saint Mark's RC Sixth Form College

Stanley Park

L4

XV

'Now, why did I do that?' I asked myself. 'Stop and sign off like I was still at St. Mark's?'

The sun had gone in. Grey afternoon light crept catlike through the library, lending the objects around me – books, shelves, desk and chair, even the 50p biro and A4 jotter I was using – a depth of seriousness that added to the highbrow glamour of both libraries – this one at Constantine's Chambers, and that one at St. Mark's.

Pictures flowed. Words too. Only one thing to do. Go forward, not back – further up and further in – into the story...

*

... Geraldine, once she had settled in, felt happier at St. Mark's than at any other time or place in her life. At first, this surprised her. Britain, after all, had been conquered and cut in two. Scotland, the North of England and North Wales were only allowed their own government on condition that they made life as easy as possible for the German High Command in London.

Ronnie DuVal, however, had been canny in the way he had set things up. He had asked the authorities in Manchester for permission to establish a college of his own at St. Mark's. His aim, he told them, was to nurture spiritual and artistic growth through teaching true British values and turning away from the errors of mind and false ideologies – liberalism, individualism and materialism – that had softened Britain from within and led to her downfall. Manchester checked with London, and the High Command gave its rubber stamp. The conquerors, as DuVal well knew, had little love for individualism, liberalism, and materialism. They viewed St. Mark's, he believed, as a harmless distraction for the British, a mock-castle where they could play 'toy soldiers' and lick their wounds. It posed no threat, and, with a little luck, might even help sway hearts and minds towards their own anti-liberal worldview.

Geraldine learned all this from DuVal himself. He liked and valued her. That was obvious. That was good. 'You were one of the very first to come,' he told her in his office, one crisp December morning. 'You came of your own will. You came, like me, because you were desperate. Unlike me, you left your family behind. But you had to. I understand. Defeat had stung you to the quick, and – unlike most others, it has to be said – you found a response in yourself. You felt compelled to come, compelled to contribute, and compelled to kick back.'

DuVal's office was high on the fourth floor. A curving bay window looked out onto sky, treetops, and – to the West – the bombsmacked pinnacles and domes of Liverpool. It was rare that he met her alone. Other facilitators were usually present – learned, experienced, high-powered men and women, all much older than Geraldine – expert in law, finance, politics, history, science, sport, and so much more that she felt she knew nothing about.

'You teach 'em English Lit,' DuVal instructed her. 'Teach 'em Shakespeare. Teach 'em intuition and vision. Without vision, you see, the people perish. That's what we were missing, Geraldine.

That's why Jerry rolled us over so easily. That's what we need. That's how we kick back.'

So, Geraldine taught *Macbeth, Richard II and The Tempest*, the only Shakespeare plays she knew. She was nervous. She wasn't much older than the punters, but DuVal had let her off the leash and given her *carte blanche* to say and do exactly as she wanted. The students loved it. They loved her. And so did Ronnie DuVal. All was well, tremendously well – despite the sting of defeat – in Geraldine's world.

Ronnie DuVal was a large, heavy-set man, with a lined, craggy face and a shaggy mane of grey hair, marked here and there with odd, striking streaks of black and white. He only seemed to have two outfits – even when he was painting – either his officer's uniform, or a pink shirt, blue serge jacket and faded jeans combination. He looked, to Geraldine, exactly like an artist should – serious and distinguished on the one hand; wild and unmanageable on the other.

When not in his office, DuVal could usually be found in his studio on the ground floor, just to the left of the chandelier, at the end of the red-carpeted hallway that welcomed teachers, students and visitors to St. Mark's. That rich, textured, mysterious paintsmell, coupled with the sight of DuVal at work, left Geraldine spellbound every time she peeped her head around the door.

Many paintings, it was clear, reflected his experience and understanding of the war. There were night-time scenes aplenty: images of silent shuttered houses, skeletal trees, and distant dispassionate stars above. There were bright, sunny depictions as well, but DuVal's boulevards were hushed, and the shops – barricaded with golden gleaming sandbags – stood empty and deserted. Offices and tower blocks burned and blazed in others, while planes trailed blood in violet skies, and ships shattered, then sank, in boiling, frothing waters.

DuVal, when working on these war paintings, often seemed possessed, Geraldine noted, by some violent inner demon. His arms whirled, his legs twitched, his head shook angrily from side to side, yet Geraldine never felt frightened or alarmed. She knew, first and foremost, that the war (lost in the outer world) was raging still in his inner world – this wrenching transmutation of defeat's humiliation and the loss of everything (except his family) he held dear into something healing, meaningful, eternal, good and true.

Duval seemed neither bothered nor distracted by Geraldine's presence at the studio door. He would never acknowledge her, but she had a feeling that he knew she was there. A bond, she sensed, was springing up between them. One day, she felt more confident, creeping into the studio itself and curling up on the floor like a cat so she could watch him close up. That was when she realised, for the very first time in her life, that she felt valued, loved and appreciated.

Geraldine's father had died when she was very young and her mother had beaten and scolded her. Her life had been unhappy. Whenever she succeeded in making friends at school or achieving sporting, scholarly or artistic success, there was always some error or misjudgement – a rash comment or an ill-timed loss of temper – that would blot out her joy and reduce her once again to a state of hapless, hopeless grasping for a happiness that seemed perpetually out of reach. She wondered, as she watched DuVal colour, with obvious distaste, a Nazi banner, what ways she could find to foul up her life at St. Mark's – the longest, deepest spell of sustained contentment and inner peace, war or no war, she had ever known.

Because, of course, the war was still roaring on, inside DuVal, for sure, but also, according to the underground papers and radio stations, all around the world. The Germans were fighting in Russia now, while the Americans continued to scope out ways to join the conflict. Resistance movements sprouted up in Ukraine, Greece, France, everywhere, it seemed, apart from Britain. 'Unless,' Geraldine asked herself, 'St. Mark's itself, despite appearances, is a centre of resistance, with Ronnie DuVal its leader?'

The more she thought about it, the less outlandish the thought seemed. Though DuVal, in his speeches and talks, continually underlined the importance of family, hierarchy and tradition – much as the Germans did – there was nothing fascistic or dictatorial in the way either he or the rest of the facilitators went about things. Geraldine had never seen any hint of discrimination against Jews, blacks, disabled people, homosexuals, or anyone who wasn't white or European.

A wide variety of views could be found among the facilitators. DuVal himself stated openly that he believed in God. Others, such as the historian, Adam Vintner, did not. The Italian sculptor, Camilla Calcanti, argued passionately for the maintenance of European civilisation, while the Portsmouth playwright, Cecylia Chung, believed it was a great evil that needed abolishing from within by the rising consciousness of the oppressed working-classes. Strangely, however, none of these differences seemed to matter that much. There was no ill feeling. No bad blood. No animosity. No back-biting. No gossip. The atmosphere at St. Mark's was harmonious and united.

'What joins us all together,' DuVal declared at supper one night, 'is a shared belief in the value and dignity of every human person. We believe in potential at St. Mark's. We believe that everyone has a calling of their own and a unique, specific role to play in the world. Our particular role, here in this building, is to step forward, without fear, into the future, while maintaining and nourishing our roots in tradition. We hope thereby to help inaugurate a world where the balance between the individual and society is right and just, and where every man and woman shines like a star at the heart of their community. Our world – the world of St. Mark's – is a world of liberty within discipline, not – as with the enemy – a world of discipline without liberty.'

From that day forth, Geraldine understood more and more the true nature and purpose of St. Mark's. It was a school for a new generation of leaders, imbuing them with the qualities they would need – practical, spiritual, artistic – to lead the country after the war, and, before that could happen, to play their own part in ridding the country of the invader.

There was one DuVal canvas in particular, on the back wall of the chapel, behind the altar, which, the more Geraldine reflected on it, completely gave the game away. It was called *The Partisans*, and it showed a group of hooded figures making their way through a mountain pass at night, their leader carrying a jewelled casket, all aglow in an unearthly blue light.

'*We* are the Partisans,' she said to herself. 'The night is the Occupation, and the blue light Liberty.'

*

'I hope we get rid of them soon,' she said aloud one rainy autumn morning, lost in a world of her own, as she skipped down the staircase to breakfast. Ronnie DuVal was standing in the hallway, under the chandelier, talking to three oily-looking men in trench coats she hadn't seen before. He shot her a sharp glance as she passed by.

'Visitors from Manchester,' was all he said over tea and toast half an hour later. 'Best sometimes keep your thoughts to yourself, Geraldine.'

Around this time, rumours began to spread concerning a resistance movement gathering strength in the South West. The atmosphere in the house began to change. Student admissions became stricter; 'visitors from Manchester' more frequent. Geraldine felt clouds start to thicken.

Ronnie DuVal was a highly prolific painter, capable, when he wanted to, of completing two or three canvases in a day. His paintings, naturally, could be found all over the house, such as his famous 'The Angels' in the old library. transformed now, of course, into a labyrinth.

In the Great Hall, where the teaching team dined every night, on the Western Wall, hung DuVal's colossal portrayal of King Arthur. Gold and silver shards exploded out from his sword and rearing horse. Every time Geraldine looked at this painting it filled her with confidence and hope. It was hard to believe in the Occupation and the lousy puppet government when face to face with such royalty and splendour.

In front of the Eastern Wall was the dais, where Ronnie DuVal, his family, the facilitators, and representatives of the student body sat each evening. A giant flag stretched out across the wall above the dais, like the French Tricolore except with the colours reversed, so, red to the left, white in the middle and blue to the right. In the centre, on the white bit, was a drawing, in gold, of a magnificent winged lion. His front right paw rested on top of an open book, and the words on the page read: PAX TIBI MARCE, EVANGELISTA MEUS.

One afternoon, that autumn of 1942, two years after her arrival at St. Mark's, Geraldine saw a door a couple of centimetres open that she had always seen shut before. The door was at the end of the hallway, past the chandelier, to the left of the stairs and the right of Ronnie DuVal's studio. She presumed it was just a cubby hole or cleaning cupboard, but she pushed it open all the same, and was amazed and astonished to find a battered, chipped stone staircase spiralling down before her. Geraldine followed the stairs, her steps illuminated by flaming braziers lashed to the walls. At the bottom, to her right, was a blank stone wall, while a few metres ahead another flight of stairs (straight this time, not spiral) led back up. To her left, however, was something different altogether, a small chapel with six wooden pews either side of a wide central aisle. At the end of the aisle was an altar, draped in cloth of gold, with two candles burning – one to the left, one to the right – and a book lying open between them. At the foot of the altar, Geraldine saw a rough-hewn stone and a bright silver sword. A long bronze spear with a blood-red tip hung clasped to the wall at the rear of the altar.

She sat down on the left-hand side of the aisle, two pews from the front. The objects on the wall and the floor fascinated her, but what compelled her most was the book on the altar. She felt sure it was to do with her, and that in some strange fashion it told the story of her life – past, present and future. She was about to get up and take a look, when a door she hadn't noticed before, behind the altar and to the left, opened with a creak and Ronnie DuVal walked through, dressed in a white robe with purple trimming at the neck and cuffs and the golden outline of a winged lion on the front. His hands bore a silver chalice. He didn't look up, didn't acknowledge Geraldine's presence, and yet *she* knew that *he* knew she was there, and even surmised that he might have left the 'cubby hole' door open on purpose. He went to the altar, held the chalice before him at eye level, then lifted it high above his head. Geraldine closed her eyes.

When she opened them again, the chalice was on the altar and Duval was holding the book up in front of him. It had a maroon cover. He read out loud…

****

Someone was standing beside me, watching me to my left. It distracted me. Put me off. I looked up. It was Jacqueline. I nearly jumped out of my seat. My biro slipped from my hand, rolled along the table and dropped down to the floor. Jacqueline bent down, picked it up and gave it me back. She was in jeans and a white, long-sleeved blouse. Her glasses were gone and her hair was down, cascading over her shoulders like a river. She stood there so tall; switched on and glowing with life. 'I apologise, Julie,' she said. 'I didn't mean to disturb you. I thought you might fancy a break.' Her hand hovered – half up, half down – like she felt tempted, almost, to start stroking my hair, but she pointed to my writing instead and took it away before I'd realised. 'You've been in a world of your own,' she said condescendingly. 'You must be inspired. Like Taliessin. I've been here all the time, but you haven't noticed me once, not even when you came in and picked up that book on the floor.'

'W-w-where were you?'

'There.'

She pointed to the next but one desk to my right. The table-lamp was on. I hadn't even clocked how dark it had got in the room. A golden halo shone around her books and piles of papers. Her black-framed glasses lay on an open page, while a faun cardigan with shiny silver buttons lay slung across the back of the chair. I shook my head in befuddlement. 'I d-didn't see you. I'm sorry.'

She pulled her chair across, sat next to me and carried on talking. 'When you came in,' she said, 'you were in your red dress. Then you went out and when you returned you were in this lovely blue tunic.'

That was the moment, there and then, that I *saw* and *knew*. Just like that.

I hated her. I despised her. THUMP THUMP THUMP went my heart, but I steadied myself, took a deep breath, and pounced like a cunning, crafty tiger:

'Have you been working as well this afternoon, Jackie?'

'Why, of course.'

'Where's *your* tunic then?'

Her neatly-shaped eyebrows shot up, and I knew that I had her. I stood up and looked down on her, but not for long, because she stood up too and was so much taller. But that didn't stop me. Even though I felt scared. I had the bit between my teeth and thought only of Caesar. 'You don't wear a tunic,' I answered for her, 'because you think it's beneath you. You think you're too clever, too grown up, for Ceasar's rules.'

'Julie, listen. There's something you need to know.'

I jabbed my finger at her chest. 'No, *you* listen. There's something *you* need to know. 'Cos there's something *I* know. This citizens's arrest bollocks. It's Ceasar, innit? That's why you didn't want me to hear. Admit it, admit it.'

'Julie, please.'

'You upper-class Judas bitch.'

I went for her, grabbing her by the shoulders, burying my head in her neck and biting down hard: once, twice, three times. She cried out. Loud and long. Hair tumbled around me. I felt good. But she was big and strong and had me by my own hair. I couldn't overpower her. No way. So I let go, shoved her as hard as I could and legged it out of the library. I was mad. Crazed. Insane. I hardly knew who I was. I ran along the hallway to the stairs, sprinted up, stood on the landing and shouted: 'We'll have a real fight soon. The fight to end all fights. At the c-consummation of the age. We'll see who's boss then.' My words echoed and rang, round and round and round, but Jacqueline did not appear.

I carried on running, right up to my room. I turned on the light, took the picture of Constantius down from the wall, flung myself onto the bed and kissed and kissed and kissed the painting over and over again, sobbing and bawling and wailing and skriking, until I was empty inside and the only thing left to do was fall asleep.

When I slept, I dreamt. We were sat around the fire again and the man in white – Dad – was reading from his book still, but I couldn't hear a word. I realised with a shock that only Jacqueline was with me, sat to my right. We were both wearing armour – chainmail and helmets – I with a sword in my right hand and she with a Roman-style shield in her left. It was painted gold, and on it was a face and a figure, a girl with dark hair, holding something bright in her hands, like a globe or a ball or a model moon or sun. There was a big building behind her, like a church or cathedral. I heard Dad's voice, out of nowhere, slashing through the silence like a sword: 'Bridget took the Stone of Destiny in her hands,' he said. 'White like crystal it shone.'

Jacqueline turned her head, our eyes met, I awoke, and the room was dark around me. I sat up. The door was closed, but the light was off. I leapt off the bed and flicked it on. The room was bright again. Someone must have come in and switched off the light, but who? Then I remembered everything that had happened – the argument, the fight, the biting, my story. My story! Shit!

I shot out of the room, flying down the stairs like a banshee. I got to the library, opened the door, and saw Jacqueline still sat there, still writing at her desk. 'Oh Jesus Christ,' I thought. But I had to get my stuff. I couldn't leave it there. I snuck up as quietly as I could, but she heard me coming and turned her head. She smiled. Faintly. But it was enough, and I was relieved. Her eyes held no hostility. I could see that. She had her glasses back on and her cardigan too. I had no idea what time it was or how long I'd been upstairs.

My work was untouched. I picked it up, bowed my head, stiffly and embarrassedly, and left the room. 'I might have thought I'd imagined all that,' I said to myself, 'if it hadn't been for that bloody big bite mark on her neck.'

XVI

'One of you will betray me,' said Caesar to Claire, exactly one week later, on Saturday November 29th. 'Do not imagine for one moment that I am unaware of this. Consciousness of destiny, both individual and collective, is the very essence of my vocation.'

My ears pricked up, but I didn't roll over or give any special sign of interest. I was lying on my back, drinking in the paintsmell, and gazing up at the studio's coffee-coloured ceiling. I turned my head ever so slightly to the right. The curtains were open. Wind and rain lashed hard. Winter was on us. Soon it would be dark.

Caesar and Claire stood in the middle of the room, in front of her latest creation, which I couldn't properly see because they were right in the way. There were twelve paintings (not counting the work-in-progress) in the space now: four lined up along the right-hand wall, four along the left, and two either side of the door. Claire had the red tunic on; her hair tied up in a chignon. She held a white-tipped brush in her right hand and stood as still as a statue as she listened. Caesar was in his grey robe and hat.

'Betrayal is in the nature of things,' he went on, 'in a world which militates, day and night, against the good, the beautiful and the true.' He pointed towards the door, and the painting of the river, dome and city. Claire tapped her paintbrush – tip tap tip – against her thigh. 'Those men on boats,' he said, 'perform the same task as ourselves – the *Dramatis Personae* at Constantine's Chambers – forging a community of adventurous spirits in the heart of a city soon to be tested by war. But meditate for a moment, Miss Falconer, please, on what might occur if the conflict, when it begins, goes badly and the enemy prevails. If, for example, these men opt to fight on as an underground, resistance movement when the citizenry wish to surrender or negotiate terms, then the pressure on the community to conform will feel absolutely immense. One of their number, almost certainly, will argue that their cause would be better served by reaching out, at least part-way, to those clamouring for peace. The leader, inevitably, will reject any notion of compromise, at which point, the individual who has seen what he believes to be a better way will become resentful and suspect that either the leader has lost touch with reality or become so doctrinaire and inflexible in his thinking that his determination to battle on, come what may, has damaged his decision-making capacity. In this fashion, Miss Falconer – wise and perceptive on its own worldly level – the seeds of the leader's downfall are sown. This is how it happened with Arthur. This is how it happened with Christ. It is a Herculean task indeed to set your face against the world's sometimes well-meaning, though always decadent drift, to construct an authentically imaginative, spiritually-orientated, alternative pole.'

Claire blew out her cheeks and whacked her brush against her leg again. Her face was as crimson as her tunic. I'd never seen her look so exasperated. 'Caesar,' she said, 'I know all this. You've said this, or something like it, every day since I came. But what does it actually have to do with art? How will it make me a better artist?'

Caesar nodded and waited a minute before responding. 'Just being in the presence of these considerations,' he said quietly, 'will sharpen and hone your artistic sensibility. You already possess the sensitivity and humility necessary to serve as a prophet and a sign of contradiction in this degenerate world. These paintings show that clearly. You are compiling a distinctive, perceptive body of work, charged with the numinous and hinting always at those deeper levels of reality primed to unfurl themselves, like banners or flags, at the consummation of the age. Take this image, for instance.'

They turned to the work-in-progress. I stretched out my legs, yawned and rolled all the way over. The ceiling tumbled by in a brown blur. Now I was lying on my right side, with Caesar and Claire three metres or so ahead.

Now, at last, I could see. And what can I say? The painting knocked me out. A dark-haired woman in a long-sleeved, charcoal-grey tunic sat writing at a desk, with bookshelves behind her and a green-eyed white and ginger cat watching on from up top. A round window to the right showed blue sky and a squadron of fighter planes lining up in an upside-down 'V'.

The woman wrote on, unflustered and unperturbed, her brown eyes clear and bright, her expression radiant and serene. It was, I swear, the most beautiful face I've seen. A halo shone around her head. I felt a lump in my throat. She looked so much like Vivi.

Caesar didn't comment directly on the picture. He only said: 'The artist walks through the world's mid-winter, carrying the lantern of life, bearing witness to past, present and future. The artist,

Miss Falconer, is the herald of a rejuvenated world – the springtime of the invisible empire and the return of the great light.'

I left shortly after that. Caesar went out, and Claire resumed her work. I'd been cooped up all day and I fancied a bit of air, despite the wind and rain. I thought I'd walk to Didsbury Library, stop there for a bit, then walk around the backstreets for a while, before heading back for 'dinner', as the evening meal – 'tea' in my book – was known at Constantine's Chambers.

I gave Claire's arm a little pinch as I left. 'In a bit,' I said. She winked, I laughed, then ran off upstairs to get my jacket, brolly, bag, and green and white striped scarf. I decided against taking my phone. I looked at it lying on the bed. Its little blue light was flashing. I'd had a text. But I wanted space. Mental as much as physical. I'd look at it later.

Back downstairs, I realised I'd nothing to read, so I popped into the library to see what I could find. I looked around nervously. I didn't want to bump into Jacqueline there again. Our exchanges at dinner during the week had been courteous enough but frosty and tense, at least on my part. I didn't want to apologise. Even though I knew I should. But no worries for now. The coast was clear. No-one in the library at all.

I had no intention of dawdling, so I picked up a pamphlet with a pink cover and black writing lying face-up on the nearest desk – *Brittania: Eurasia's Western Pivot*, by Ambroisus Carlisle. 'That'll do,' I thought.

Whenever I wanted a break from the house, Didsbury Library (plus the Holy Name now and again) was where I headed to. The reading room, that Saturday afternoon, had the same clientele as always – a slightly uneasy mix of old fellas reading papers and giggly, distractable Sixth Form types. The pointy, patterned windows were navy blue already with approaching night. I twizzled open a bottle of 'Summer Fruits' *Oasis* and started to read. *Phoenix Fire* was the first chapter's heading.

'Europe today,' I read, 'approaches zero hour; a revelatory paroxysm of catastrophe and rebirth. The current dispensation teeters on the brink of collapse: this shameful parody, this dour, godless realm of bankers, bureaucrats, opportunists, technocrats and ladder-climbers. The age of the sham-philosophers – Foucault, Derrida, *et al* – those without imagination, those who deny our continent's Judeo-Christian, Greco-Roman heritage is, mercifully, drawing to a close. It has, however, fulfilled its mission to a 't': softening, weakening and undermining Europe from within. Radical Islam stands at the gates, poised, as in the days of the Umayyad Caliphate, to pick up the spoils.

'Europe has turned her back on the ancient, eternal light: witnessed first in Israel, articulated in Greece, then represented by Rome, Christendom and the genius of Elizabethan England. A vacuum is all that remains, a vacuum to be filled by...'

I felt a hand on my shoulder. A whisper in my ear. 'Pretty brutish stuff, isn't it, Julie?'

The pamphlet fell from my hands like a hot coal. A lad with a silly quiff and big headphones watched on with a smirk, nudging his mate who paid no attention, preferring the squiggles and lines of his Maths text book.

'It's what I tried to tell you last week,' she added.

I didn't turn around. I knew who it was. I only wished she'd shut up and go away.

XVII

She wore a green duffel coat and a blue and red tartan scarf. Her hair was up. We both held brollies in our left hands, but it looked like we mightn't need them now. The rain had stopped. But the wind bellowed and blew, beating up spray. We walked across the library forecourt and turned left. People looked silly, blown all over the place, struggling to stand up in the gale. Over the road, the lights of the cafes and bars glowed snug and enticing. Men watched football in the 'Station' pub to our left. We waited for a couple of 4 x 4s in the Aldi driveway to pass, then carried on down Wilmslow Road, the hubbub and noise of the Village behind us. I was determined not to be the first one to speak. But in the end I was. I think I felt, deep down, like I had to. There was no escape.

'I'm sorry,' I said. 'About last week. I was out of order. I don't know what came over me.'

Jacqueline laughed. 'Don't worry about it,' she said, squeezing my shoulder. 'It's nothing. Anyway, it's me who should apologise. I disturbed your flow. Did you finish your piece in the end?'

'No. I've lost the thread. It'll come back though. It always does.'

The pavement humped up before us. A yellow tramstreak whizzed by beneath, under the bridge to my left. Now the road felt wide and spacious; cars and buses well-spaced out. Rooms twinkled.

I saw a grey-haired woman chilling on a *chaise longue* with a glass of red in her hand, sharing a joke with someone I couldn't see.

We turned left onto Parkfield Road. Trees reared tall and spare, shaking down moisture. Sopping mounds of leaves lay slimy on the ground. Street lights shone in haloes of white.

'I'd like to tell you a bit about myself, Julie, if that's alright.'

'Yeah, 'course.'

'I was brought up in Provençe, in a château just outside Avignon. My father's English and my mother's French. He met her in Marseille, when he was working there.'

'What does he do?'

'He's an economic forecaster.'

'Ah.'

The street arched up, as on Wilmslow Road. I glanced to the left, thinking I might see another tram, but all I clocked was a ginger flash, like a bolt of horizontal lightning, scooting across the tracks from left to right, then burying itself in mossy banks of undergrowth.

'Was that a moggy?' I asked.

'Pardon.'

'A cat.'

'A cat? Oh yes, I think it was.'

Two parked-up taxi drivers, one on either side of the road, conducted a quiet, dignified conversation in a foreign language.

'Father's had many clients over the years,' Jacqueline resumed. 'General Motors, the Conservative Party, some of the largest financial houses in France.' She sighed. With genuine sadness, I felt.

'Father and Ambrosius Carlisle were good friends when I was a child. Very good friends. I've known Carlisle a long time, you see, Julie. He was my private tutor – in English and History. He lived in Nîmes. That's how he made his living. They'd still be friends today, if he – Carlisle, that is – hadn't stolen a bunch of Medieval antiques from our lumber room: a spear, a sword, a chalice and a stone. He returned to Britain shortly after, and neither mother nor father have seen him since.'

'You've come to get them back?' I quizzed, doing my best to sound calm.

'Ye-es, but it isn't a case of family honour. Not in the slightest. My parents aren't actually all that bothered, though father seems to have woken up a little of late to Carlisle's true nature. The antiques are just trinkets to them. Curiosities. They've so much money they don't care. They think Carlisle was jolly rude. Nothing more. But *I* care. *I'm* bothered. I know what he wants them for, you see.'

'What's that then?'

We turned left onto Elm Road. The houses were big and silent. Very few lights. Big pools of dark.

'The Templars,' Jacqueline replied, taking me by surprise, 'were very active around Avignon, you know. There are a lot of castles and fortifications. Some credulous locals believe that our antiques formed part of a supposed Templar treasure, hidden away after the order's dissolution in 1312.'

'The Templars? Who're they?'

'An order of Christian knights. Formed in the Crusades. They became very powerful; militarily and financially. Too much so, both for the Pope and the King of France. That's why they were disbanded and their Grand Master, Jacques de Molay, burned at the stake.'

'Blimey.'

'Quite.'

We were drifting off-topic. Time to cut to the chase. 'Is Caesar a Templar then?' I asked.

'Good question. There are certainly similarities between Templars and Chlorians. The point, however, is that there are one or two even more credulous types who regard our chalice as the Holy Grail itself, with the spear, sword and stone invested with the same sacred power. Ambrosius Carlisle, I am sorry to say, is foremost among their number.'

We turned left again, this time onto Barlow Moor Road. The comeback of cars and buses after the contemplative quiet of the last two streets made me blink and squint. Jacqueline slipped her hand inside the crook of my arm. 'Now, listen, Julie. This is going to sound incredible, but it is the absolute truth. I have conducted extensive research, both at King's' (I still wasn't sure if that meant London or Cambridge) 'and in France. The bottom line is this. Ambrosius Carlisle, throughout the last two decades or so – since the fall of the Soviet Union, basically – has established a network of far-right connections all over Europe. He is what is known politically as a Eurasian, and his goal is a neo-authoritarian, semi-fascist

Imperium, stretching from Galway to Vladivostok, with the Russian President ruling the East, and himself the West.'

'Whaaaat?' I laughed out loud. I'd never heard anything so daft in all my life. Totally off the scale. But Jacqueline took her arm from mine and stood in front of me. Her face was white and earnest. 'Don't underestimate him,' she said, wagging her finger like a bossy-boots teacher. 'Just because he isn't in the papers doesn't mean he isn't influential. He believes the Grail, as he imagines it to be, gives him a direct line to God and the authority to advise his friends in Moscow and other terrorist states to start a war, bring about the end of this age – the Iron Age, he calls it – and usher in a new one – the supposed Golden Age.'

She clenched and unclenched her fists. I'd never seen her looking so aryated. 'We have to stop him. Fast. He intends to act soon. How and in what way we do not know, but these troubles in the Middle East and the ex-Soviet space encourage him to think the time is near. There literally isn't a moment to lose.'

'Who's *we*?' I queried, sensing an intruder.

'Why, Rommie, of course. He's no time for Carlisle either and is happy to help me in a citizen's arrest.'

'Ah, yes, a citizen's arrest. I remember you saying. When?'

'December 21st. At the revue. We'll catch him in an act of hate-speech, no doubt concerning Islam or LGBT, and we'll arrest him from there.'

I shook my head and walked away as quickly as I could but Jacqueline's super-long legs ate up the ground and she'd caught me up in no time. So I turned and gave her a mouthful instead. 'What's it to do with me anyway? You didn't want me to hear what you said a couple of weeks ago, and now you've come to find me in the library to tell me. What is it with you? What's wrong with you?'

What she said next floored me. Just like Claire's painting. 'Because you're in danger, Julie. It's become clear that he believes you are chosen to follow him closely, a little like the beloved discile in John's Gospel, if you know that piece of fiction. It's probably why he's so hung up on this Taliessin business.'

'M-m-me? Why?'

Jacqueline held up her hand. The traffic whizzing by made her look like a policewoman. An older lady with a little cocker spaniel walked past from the direction of the Village. The dog jumped on Jacqueline's leg for a second. It was comical and made her look rather foolish. 'Thank you, Mr. Dog,' she bantered lamely. 'Now go away please.' But she swiftly recovered her composure. 'We don't know, Julie. But it *is* a fact. Our spies have seen a book he keeps with the Grail – not the one he reads to us from sometimes, but a book of symbols and images. It tells stories in pictorial form. He believes that one of the characters is you.'

'How? Why? How do you know all this?'

'Well, he told your teacher, David Martin, for a start.'

'You been earwigging his phone calls?'

'Yes. Emails as well.'

'Jesus.'

I left it at that. The mention of 'spies' unsettled me, but I'd a sense, despite her bluster, that she didn't know yet that I'd actually seen the Grail. Unless Claire had told her, but Claire didn't like her – 'She's so stuck up,' Claire said – so that was a no-no. It was nice to have one ace, at least, that I could pin to my chest.

'It's highly likely,' she droned on, 'that Carlisle may, in the next few days, ask you to take a plane to Moscow to set certain events in motion. You are on no account to go.'

'Don't tell me what to do,' I hissed, peering at her through my fringe and the misty rain that had started up again.

'Julie, please.'

'Why are you here anyway? Why has he let you come if you're just out to get him?'

Jacqueline's eyes, beneath her glasses, narrowed to a pair of brown beady points. 'I'm not out to get him. I'm here to save him and us from the anger he feels towards the establishment for rejecting him. Listen, Julie, Carlisle's an inspirational, out-of-this-world teacher. I should know. But his intellect needs to be chanelled. At the moment, it's warped. And right now, I'm afraid, he's displaying all the symptoms of advanced megalomania. One minute he's Augustus Caesar, the next King Arthur, with you as his Virgil or Taliessin. Can't you see how dangerous it all is? He's a menace, Julie: to himself, to us, and now to the world. We have to arrest him. It's far from ideal, but there's no other way. From there we can rehabilitate him and find a *milieu* for his many talents.'

'You've not answered my question.'

She threw up her hands, like I was a stroppy, temperamental kid. 'For goodness sake, Julie. Do you think I take any pleasure in lying and deceiving? He's welcomed me to his house in good faith. King Duncan to my Macbeth. He believes, if you insist on knowing, that I'm here simply to re-establish our old relationship. The fact that I'm EU sponsored gives him a little more Kudos, and also he's said that he sees me as a challenge, and that he wants to cure me of my atheism. Well, that's not going to happen. He's no idea why I'm here. None at all. Fortunately for us, in the immediate term at least, he's too bound up in grandiose geopolitical scheming to see beyond the end of his nose.'

I groaned inside. I recognised a sad, but nonetheless irresistible logic to what she was saying. Jacqueline, whatever her faults, had no selfish motives. I could see that. No greed or lust for gain. She was on the side of right. We were nearly home now anyway. Grenfell Road lay opposite in fact. I gave in. 'Come to my room for a bit, if you want,' I said.

'I'd love to. But I said I'd meet Rommie at six.'

I kept quiet. 'She'll ask me to come along,' I thought. She didn't.

'I'll think about what you said then. I'll let you know.'

'Thank you Julie.'

I was already crossing the road. I was in no mood to hang around.

I couldn't settle when I got back. Constantine's Chambers was like a ghost town. All the lights were on, but no-one was around. I could smell some kind of goulash or stir-fry cooking in the kitchen, but the door was shut and I felt for some reason that it'd be somehow inappropriate or remiss of me to enter. I lay on the bed, dozed for a bit, then decided to try and do some writing, though I didn't much feel like it in truth. I was all confused and unsettled. I put on a tunic – red with a gold star – and sat at the desk. But nothing would come. I had simply no idea how to conclude my story. I was thinking too much. I got up and went to the toilet.

There are (or were), I should have said by now, four rooms on our corridor as you come up from the stairs and turn left: Camilla's, mine, Claire's and Jacqueline's. The shower area is just past Jacqueline's. Caesar and the boys live on the parallel corridor, while Lolek and Glinka have the outhouse in the garden.

Therefore, to get to the toilet, I had to walk past Claire's room first, then Jacqueline's. So, I walked past Claire's room. I knew where she was. Expo. No signs or sounds of life from her room then.

I thought I knew where Jacqueline was as well. The Sevastopol Suite. Yet I *did* hear noises from her room. Horrific noises. The door, I saw, hung a little ajar. A hot red glow stole through.

I heard a voice from Heaven, I swear I did: 'Stop. Come no closer.' But I paid no heed. I knew it was wrong. I knew that I shouldn't. I just couldn't stop. Compelled, sucked in, closer, closer, closer. I gave the door a push, just a little at first, then a bit more, then a bit more still, and there they were. I'd known it all along.

Naked on the bed. I could see them, but they couldn't see me. Romulus had a Celtic Cross tatoo on his back. 'You don't deserve that symbol,' I said aloud. But he didn't hear. Jacqueline had her legs wrapped around his muscly shoulders. She had a silver bracelet on her left ankle, which (obviously) I hadn't seen before. I couldn't see her face.

I crumbled, fell apart, broke up, dissolved. I could look no longer. At the foot of the bed, a pile of clothes: green coat, tartan scarf, glasses, t-shirt, jeans, other bits and bobs...

Jacqueline cried out, and my soul snapped like a twig. I turned and ran and was sick in the toilet – *bleughhh, bleughhh, bleughhh.* I ran back, open-mouthed in silent-scream, hands covering my ears, as if what I might hear might condemn me, if I'd not been condemned already, to all eternity in the fires of Hell.

Back in my room I went straight to my books and flung the whole lot of the shitty things full blast against the walls. *Prince Caspian*, SPLAT; *The Last Battle*, CRASH; *The Silver Chair,* BLAT; *The Lantern Bearers,* SMASH. I literally ripped the pages out of *Ulysses*, pretentious hunk of shit. Then, for good measure, I picked up my phone, lying harmlessly on the bed, and smashed that into a gazillion pieces too. 'Fucken' useless things,' I shouted. 'I knew it all along. All my life. And I ran away and hid. In storybooks and childish things.' I tore and rent my tunic and cried and moaned and rolled around on the bed for hours and hours on end. Eventually I got up, turned off the light and buried my head in the pillow and darkness. I fell asleep. And didn't dream. When I woke up I'd no idea what time it was. The rain was hammering on the window. But my mind was sharp and clear. I felt burnt-out inside. Pecked clean. I was empty. A blank slate. But not in a bad way. Not bad at all. I had my story. At last, I had my story ...

****

... I, Geraldine, met with DuVal in the Great Hall for the last time on the night the Germans brought fire to the Unoccupied Zone. I never learnt if we were betrayed or not. But Chester had fallen, and St. Mark's would be next.

There were no students anymore. Just DuVal, myself and five other facilitators. Everyone else had fled. On the wall, behind his head, was a tapestry I hadn't seen before – a red and golden Phoenix rising from the flames and ashes.

DuVal stood before us in the candlelight, the old winged-lion flag in one hand and a bright long-handled knife in the other. And the flag was cut – solemnly, sacramentally – into seven shining pieces, one for each of us.

'Keep these fragments close to your hearts,' he said. 'One day we will meet again, here or elsewhere. The flag will be made whole. Logres will be restored.'

At midnight, when the *Wermacht* came, we dispersed in seven different directions. I ran and ran – wind streaming my hair, light sparking my eyes – until the shooting started and I heard DuVal cry out. I stopped. I turned. I saw. My soul snapped like a twig.

*

It took me all night, crawling back to where he lay. But I came too late. He was a mess of wounds. And all those things I wanted to tell him, needed to tell him...

I slid my hand into the pocket of his greatcoat, dragging out his fragment of flag – red and white on one side, with a strange, childlike drawing in gold and silver crayon on the other. It was a Phoenix rising from the flames and ashes. And the face of the Phoenix was my own.

*

Gunfire crackled. I left him. I had to. I carried on crawling, through the garden, to the secret tunnel. If there was one thing I could do for Ronnie DuVal, then this was it – to take the treasures I'd seen in his secret chapel. I had a strong sense that the Germans would prize them highly. I had no idea if they had power in themselves or not, but I knew that they were sacred to DuVal, and that was good enough for me. There was no way I was going to let them be sullied by Nazi hands.

I feared the worst long before the tunnel straightened out. No light, not even a flicker. The chapel was dark and cold. The candles were out, and the sword, spear, chalice and stone gone. As was the book.

Blackness and desolation descended upon me. They remain with me now, and will always be with me, yes, to the end of time. For I have lost my father for the second time. I have lost my chief, *mon chef*, the man who brought meaning, purpose and direction to my life. For I have failed him. Three times over. I failed to bury him. I failed to guard his treasures. I failed to pour out my heart to him.

What care I now if Hitler wins the war? DuVal was there for me. I wasn't there for him. I came too late, swanning down the street with a lolly-ice in my gob while he lay dying. Now the iron chains fasten and tighten. Now the devils mock. They have me now. Forever. For I have failed. They are taking me down now, to those dark regions where the fires burn and horned figures dance and rage with whips and pitchforks in the heart of the burning blaze. Naked, glistening figures lie twisted in flames beside me. They are taking me to them now. This is my home. This is where I belong. For I have always been here. Before the beginning of the world, and after its end. For all eternity I have been here.

****

'You will have to change your conclusion, *Mith* Carlton. Too gloomy. Too *pethimithtic*.'

'B-but Caesar, there's a plot. I've just told you.'

He waved his hand dsimissively. 'Bah. I know all that. I told you that this afternoon, didn't I? In the studio with Miss Falconer.'

He handed me back the jotter. 'Go and work on the ending. Everything else is excellent. But we don't give way to despair, Miss Carlton. Not at Constantine's Chambers.'

I'd found him in the library, sat, funnily enough, in the seat Jacqueline had been in the Saturday before. I told him everything. Well, not quite everything. I left out the bit about Jacqueline and

Romulus, though I think he could tell that something had upset me. My torn and battered tunic bore witness to that.

There was no-one else in the library. Outside, the storm had kicked up again. But inside, the table-lamps cast an orange comforting glow. Caesar was in the same black robe as I'd seen him in on my first day. He didn't seem rattled at all by what I said. He listened, nodded, said 'mm, yes' from time to time, and generally looked on top of things. He'd been reading a book when I came in. His black felt hat lay next to it. It had a black leather cover and gold lettering on the spine. I pointed to it. 'I'm sorry, Caesar,' I said. 'You were reading. I disturbed you. I apologise.'

'Not at all, Miss Carlton. You have done the right thing, believe me. It is exactly what I would have expected of you.'

He leant his bushy head towards mine, speaking quietly, almost in a whisper. 'I would, as it happens, like you, if possible, to perform a certain favour for me please. Not flying to Moscow, perhaps, but rather – in case of such incidents as Miss Cutter speaks – to take charge of the Grail and its Hallows and conduct them to a place of safe-keeping. It is absurd, of course, to speak of Augustus Caesar being arrested or held captive in any way, but if an attempt is made against our person, then I will have to travel lightly. I believe and know that I can count on you, Miss Carlton. You have earned my trust and admiration.'

I was made up with that. Chuffed to bits. 'Thank you Caesar,' I said.

He sat back, took up a green fountain pen, twiddled it around a bit, put it down, grimaced, sighed and spoke, his blue eyes bright but angry: 'There's so much nonsense talked about Augustus Ceasar, there really is, you know. It maddens me. Absolutely maddens me. Miss Cutter means well, of course she does. I am sure that you have gathered that already. But her defence of rationalism and Enlightenment values is as narrow and one-sided as the religious and political fundamentalism she so rightly decries.

'Now, look, Miss Carlton. I am not a progressive. I admit that. I don't read *The Guardian* or *Libération* or *The Tablet* or anything like that. I am not a rationalist either. Nor even a liberal. But that does not mean I am some kind of dictator in waiting. I am not a fascist, not even a semi-fascist, as she puts it. I abhor fascism, just as I abhor all *math* movements. I am a Chlorian; a traditionalist; an aristocrat of the spirit. There is a quantum intellectual and spiritual leap between that and fascism. You only have to look at the history of Germany to see the extent to which the Nazis and the German aristocratic warrior class were so often at odds.'

'But you're not into democracy either, Caesar?'

'I have told you. I am a royalist. I believe in a natural, organic hierarchy, as I told you on your first day.'

He lobbed me the pen. I caught it, giggled, and chucked it him back. He laughed. 'The key, as always, Miss Carlton, is imagination, or the lack of it in this case. Miss Cutter, for all her academic prowess, lacks imagination. She is a literalist – one dimensional and wooden in her judgements. Unable to see outside the square, and think and act creatively.'

'Why have you let her come then, Caesar?'

'Because this is her time. This is her hour. These things need to be. Listen, I have been in education for a long time. My days here may well be numbered. It might well be time for a new creative phase in my life. If she brings this place down, then fine. How Ceasar responds, as always, will be what counts.'

I remembered what Jacqueline had said about 'friends' in Moscow. 'Do you know the Russian President, Caesar?'

'Pah,' he said. 'I know many people with a passion for remodelling the continent and restoring its grandeur – some well known; some not. What does it matter who I know?'

'What about gay people? Jackie said something about LGBT and that you might make some kind of hate-speech remark at the revue.'

He looked at me coldly, his eyes two block of ice. 'Miss Cutter, I regret to say, has overstepped the mark there. That is a barefaced lie, and typical of the blanket condemnation the chattering classes throw at anyone who diverges from their pre-packaged world view. My opinion of Anthony Cutter's daughter has declined, I regret to say. When I select a student, Miss Carlton, I can assure you that their sexuality is very far from my thinking.'

'What about Islam, Caesar? Do you select Muslims too?'

He flung out his arms, incredulity written all over his face. 'Of course I do. Bloody Hell. If Miss Cutter knew as much as she claims, she would know all about my connections in the Shia world, particularly Iran.' He leant forward again, calming down a bit. 'I should tell you, Miss Carlton, that I greatly admire the emphasis placed by the Shia on mysticism and the interior contemplative light of imagination – the *mundus imaginalis*, as the scholar, Henry Corbin has it. Do you know, as an aside, what the word 'Shia' actually means?'

I shook my head.

'It means 'partisans'. The Shia are the partisans, and that is how I feel sometimes, hemmed in by fundamentalists and literalists of all types: political, religious, scientific...'

'And yet you've criticised Islam, Caesar. You've said it's banging at the gates of Europe.'

'So I have, my child, and so it is. But you will note that when I speak of the religion in this context, I use the prefix 'radical'. Now this 'radical' Islam, or Islamism, as it is sometimes known, is a gross subversion of the holy revelation given to the Prophet, peace be upon him. It latches on to Islam, and we have to fight it tooth and nail, wherever it rears its Hydra head. In truth, however, it owes far more to the mass movements of the modern era than either Sunni or Shi'ite spirituality. Think of the Jacobins in revolutionary France, or the Bolsheviks, or the Nazis. Yes, especially the Nazis.'

Someone knocked on the door. Lolek popped his head around. 'A visitor for Miss Julie,' he announced, before disappearing again.

'For me? Who'd want to s-see me?'

Caesar stood up and patted me on the shoulder. 'Receive your visitor here,' he said. 'We can resume our conversation afterwards. In the Grail Chapel, if you wish. There is something I would like to show you.'

He left the room. 'Oh wow,' I thought. 'The Grail Chapel.'

I sat there for a long time, it seemed, without much happening. I heard muffled voices outside, one male (Caesar) and one female (my 'visitor', I presumed). I couldn't hear what was said. The door opened. A tall young woman stood looking at me with wide, round, very brown eyes. She wore slim-fitting jeans, blue and white Puma trainers and a red Adidas top, all shiny and wet, with black stripes down the arms. I had no idea who she was. She had close-cropped black hair and was as beautiful as the woman in Claire's picture, so beautiful I couldn't look for long and had to turn away.

'Jules,' she said, and I knew her by her voice. I shot up from my chair and ran across the room. 'Oh, Vivi, Vivi,' I cried, folding my arms around her and hugging, hugging, hugging. 'You're so tall,' I babbled. 'How could I ever have thought she was taller?'

'Hush, Jules,' was all she said, as she ran her fingers through my hair. 'Hush, Jules.'

****

Ma was ill. Critically ill. In the Heart and Chest Hospital, in fact. Father Fox had already been, and that's why Vivi had come. She'd texted me in the day, but I hadn't looked at it, of course. She'd called me too, but I'd smashed up the phone by then. She'd emailed me during the week, but I'd stopped going online as soon as I got to Constantine's Chambers. I'd wanted nothing to get in the way of my imaginative flow, and now here I was, packing my sports bag and leaving, though I knew it was just for a while, and that at least I'd finished my story. Apart from the end anyway.

On a whim, I decided to take the painting of Constantius and the silver-haired woman too. I was sure Caesar wouldn't mind, and it would do as a reminder of things for however long I was away.

I looked around. 'Bye room, I said. 'See you soon.' Then I saw that someone had stuffed a note under my door. I crouched down, unfolded it and had a shufty:

I should also have said, Julie, that his name is not *Ambrosius Carlisle. That is a 'non de plume'.* His real name is Russell Paul.

Speak soon, J x

'Oh, piss off,' I thought, as I locked the door and went downstairs.

Vivi had come in her orange mini. I could hear it staring up outside. I got in, fell asleep, and woke to a shock of mist and spray, as the halogen-lit, tarmac river of the M62 bore me back home, and away from what I suddenly and shockingly realised was the totally 'insubstantial pageant', as Prospero says in *The Tempest*, of Constantine's Chambers.

XVIII

'Izzit yer Mah, Joolz?'

It's funny how you bump into people you know in the weirdest locations.

'Awww, bless you, darling.'

Gemma Hastings squeezed me tight and kissed me on the cheek.

'Thanks Gem,' I said.

The nurse's uniform suited her – grey with white piping. Her brown curly hair was piled up high, almost in a beehive. She had so much rouge on her cheeks it looked like she'd had her head stuck in an oven for an hour.

People are good to you when you're bereaved. I hadn't seen Gem since we'd left Mount Carmel. We hadn't been all that close either. Yet she treated me with such love and tenderness. Like I was her sister. I could tell by the tears ready to roll in her eyes.

Vivi came out of the doctor's office. She shook his hand. He looked like one of the taxi drivers I'd walked past with Jacqueline earlier. It was time to go.

'I'm just a student,' said Gemma, like I'd put her on the spot, even though I hadn't. 'I've only just started. I've ages to go.'

'Ah, you'll be fine,' I called back as we left. 'You're a natural.'

She smiled and waved, like she was seeing me off from Lime Street.

We walked through the car park. 'Christ, what a night,' I reflected, as we zigzagged around the cars and avoided the punters shuttling in and out of the hospital. So many normal things seemed to be still going on: staff chatting, people having a smoke at the gates, cars and buses rattling past. It couldn't even have been that late. Maybe not even midnight. The air was cool and fresh. No storms in Liverpool.

'If I'd have gone to the bookies this afternoon,' I ruminated, 'I wouldn't have got five thousand to one on the day panning out like this. I'd have been laughed out of town.'

I stayed two and a half weeks in the end. Miles longer than I'd anticipated. I only came back to Constantine's Chambers this morning, in fact – Wednesday December 17th – though it seems like a million years ago now.

That's the freaky thing. Last night I slept in my old room on Canning Street. Tonight I don't know where I am. 'Things fall apart', as Caesar said that first day...

It was a sad time, for sure, but a reflective time too. Ma's funeral was a week last Monday: December 8th. She had chronic emphysema, complicated by liver issues. Once I'd understood, deep down, that she was definitely gone, I felt so guilty, wretched and irresponsible for leaving her. 'It's all my fault,' I told everyone who'd listen, but everyone, basically, told me to shut up, chill out and stop giving myself a hard time. Ma was beyond help, really. No-one said it like that, of course, but that's what they meant. In my heart, I think I agreed.

She had a good turnout at least. All my friends who were still in Liverpool came, even Donna and Martina, which was nice. Billy was there too, and Gina popped back specially from Leeds, which was lovely. I found Father Fox a lot less annoying than at Dad's funeral. He conducted the service slowly, with dignity and reverence. His white robe went well, I felt, with his red 'drinker's' face. I'm not sure if he'd been as deliberate and purposeful at Dad's funeral. Maybe he liked Ma more? I don't think I noticed that much anyway when Dad died. I was too blinded with grief to care about anything.

Gavin, Ma's 'friend', was there as well, as I'd expected, his browny-grey hair assaulted by Brylcreem, as he shuffled and wriggled around in his unaccustomed suit and tie get-up. I clocked him going out for a ciggie straight after Communion, when there was still a fair bit to go, but despite that, I actually found him quite charming and totally harmless. I couldn't work out why I'd been so mad at him earlier in the year. He was just another alky really – more to be pitied, and helped where possible, than hated or seen as an enemy.

It had been a strange experience, sat in the front pew with just my sister for company. It made me realise how incredibly small our family is. Neither Ma nor Dad ever mentioned having brothers or sisters or any kind of extended family, which is unusual (so I'm told) in Irish households. I'm not sure either of us ever thought to ask further, certainly not me. I just took the absence of uncles and aunts as part of the natural order of happy childhood things. What you don't have, you don't miss, and all that.

I definitely didn't miss having a big family during those two and bit weeks in Liverpool. I was grateful for the peace and quiet. It's a funny thing. Even though Canning Street is much closer to Liverpool centre than Didsbury is to Manchester, it still feels a lot quieter. There's less bustle. Less hubbub. I'm not sure why that is, but I realised, especially after the funeral, that I'd been aware of that extra level of quiet before I'd left and that I'd missed it, perhaps without realising, while I'd been away.

In some ways, my time back home reminded me of the spell at Constantine's Chambers between my arrival and the night I first heard the phrase, 'citizen's arrest.' I had the same still, restful vibe, but without the distraction of Romulus and The Sevastopol Suite and all that silliness and over-heated nonsense with Jacqueline.

By the time I got to last Wednesday, I'd decided not to go back to Constantine's Chambers. Viewed from half-way along Canning Street, the house and everything associated with it seemed so infantile and daft. Ambrosius Carlisle, or 'Caesar', as I'd fallen into the trap of calling him there, seemed to me now like an over-grown schoolboy, playing what Jacqueline had called 'pre-pubescent ego games'. She'd been spot on too in what she'd said about Carlisle projecting his resentment at academia onto the whole world. It seemed obvious from this distance, under grey, but not unfriendly skies, with my old (and nearly fully forgiven) ally, the Anglican tower, watching on from the end of the street.

It seemed clear to me too that Jacqueline herself had a number of issues, an inferiority complex most likely, probably pertaining to her high-powered parents. She was just as much of an egotist as Carlisle, possibly more so, blathering on about 'spies' and 'Moscow' and what have you, like she'd been reading too many John le Carré books. I saw how they needed each other – herself and Carlisle – and how each gave value and meaning and a sense of conflict and drama to the stories they spun about themselves – their equivalent of my 'myths and legends', if you like. That was why she had gone there, and that was why he had taken her on. It was all a game. Unconscious, of course, but still a game. They saw themselves both as standing at the heart of some tremendous epic upon which the whole fate of the world depended. How pathetic. How totally pathetic. How had I managed to get myself caught up in such upper-class charades? Silly pricks. Same with the acting group (except maybe Jean-Luc), those self-absorbed 'theatre practioners', in Jim's horrendous phrase. 'What a bunch of show-ponies,' I concluded. 'If I could transplant Claire, Lolek and Glinka here, then I think I'd be perfectly happy forever. The rest I've no time for. I don't want to see the spankers again.'

Vivi had kitted up the house exceptionally nice. She had actually been there for the whole two weeks preceding Ma being taken to hospital. That meant she was behind on her course a bit, so she spent a lot of time, during the days, in town at the library, writing in cafés like a proper arty, and working on her thesis, which I think was to do with St. Teresa of Avila and her mystical book, *The Interior Castle*.

I was quite happy just staying in, to be honest. I didn't really fancy going out, not even to revisit the old routes that Dad used to walk me round. I think, in some ways, there was part of me that wanted to get away from all that and 'move on', as it were. As I'd already realised, the night I'd seen that reprehensible pair together, it was time I grew up and started putting 'childish things aside', as St. Paul says.

The house, as I say, was in any case lovely. Vivi had cleaned it spick and span. Stripped down and stylish. It held no ghosts for me, no oppressive memories, and no real nostalgia either. There were no pictures now (except in Vivi's little box-room 'chapel') and I was glad of that. It gave me time and space to think; whether I was sitting at the wooden kitchen table, looking out onto the yard; or lounging about in the front room, bouncing up and down on the black springy sofa; or sat in the living room in the super-comfy wicker chair Vivi had bought to replace Dad's (and Gavin's) armchair. It made me understand too that there'd probably been too much clutter in my life, in terms of books, stories, pictures, ideas, and so forth, and that I might be better served in future with clarity and simplicity in my head rather than a teeming mass of themes and images culled from a mish-mash of myths and legends from Ireland, Greece, Britain, Rome, and all kinds of random places. Not that I was angry with Dad, or felt that he shouldn't have done what he did, but that it had its time in my life and that now it was time for something different. Something new. A fresh start. A blank canvas.

I started to work out a plan. I'd apply to Uni for the next academic year, or even the one after if I was cutting it a little fine now. I decided not to consider Liverpool, only because it'd weird me out a bit going to Uni in my own city, yet surrounded by people probably from down South in the main. But I'd do the next best thing and go to somewhere very like Liverpool – so, Newcastle maybe (even though that was, of course, Ambrosius Carlisle's home town), Glasgow, or Bristol perhaps, even though that last one was possibly a bit far away. In the end, I settled for Durham, which, I know, is nothing at all like Liverpool, but it's got so much going for it that I couldn't possibly turn it down – a bit of old-world academic class, close (but not too close) to Newcastle, a knock-out cathedral, and bang on the train line to boot, so I could nip back to the centre of the world whenever I wanted. I'd no idea where I'd stay or who I'd stay with when I'd come back, but I was determined to keep the friends I already had here and treat them better and with more respect than I'd done before.

Talking of which, I went down to Soul Cafe with Billy for a coffee last week. It went okay – a bit stilted here and there – but generally okay. I think he still likes me. I might be wrong, but that's the vibe I get. He's definitely forgiven me. He's a good lad. He wouldn't have bought me that chocolate cake if he hadn't!

I'm still not sure really if I want to 'go out' with him, but I think I could work on it perhaps and at least give it a go. He's my own age and my own type and I've known him for years. God, I was so up my arse with all that baloney I said about 'men' and 'boys' in Chapter VI. Delusions of grandeur once more.

While I was out with Billy, I ran into Thomasina Brakespeare, the Café Manager at FACT. She basically offered me my old job back, but though I said I would, I secretly thought I wouldn't. I'd had enough of the Arts, to be honest. I wanted to have a word with Vivi and see if I could get involved in some kind of work with disabled kids or something. It was time, I felt, that I started putting something back into the city and stopped swanning around on 'Planet Julie' with my head in the clouds. I promised myself I'd start properly going to Mass as well, and try and get over myself and all that fuss I made about busy churches and people standing and sitting and kneeling and doing my head in. I felt I needed to make more of an effort and tune myself in to something bigger, wider, deeper and older than myself (the Church), rather than try to make God Himself and all the angels and saints revolve around little Planet Julie.

The only other thing I wanted to do, so I could begin with a proper clean slate, was pop over to St. Mark's and have a chat with Mr. Martin and Dr. Tenby, just to let them know how I'd got on (an edited version, most likely) and where my head was at now. One of them would be pleased and one disappointed, I figured, but what could I do? I had to stop living my life according to what others (however well-meaning and wise) expected or wanted of me.

I didn't get chance in the end to go. But even after Vivi had talked me into going back to CC, I wasn't too concerned. I'd agreed with her, you see, that I'd only go back till the December revue had come and gone. 'I'll see 'em soon enough,' I said to myself. Vivi was of the opinion that I had to honour my commitment to Carlisle until the 'citizen's arrest' threat had passed. She also surprised me by saying that, if the worst came to the worst, I should take the 'Hallows' and let her take them to London. She'd find somewhere safe for them, she said. I was intrigued. She'd certainly changed her tune from the summer when she warned me over and over to have nothing to do with Constantine's Chambers. As with Jacqueline in The Sevastopol Suite that time, I felt something afoot behind that calm, devout exterior. But what?

Vivi had changed a great deal, it seemed to me. She was quieter on the whole and more serious and intent in her prayer life. She'd get up every morning at five, go to her chapel and pray for an hour before the start of each day. Sometimes, I'd join her. She'd put a couple of Eastern-style icons up – an image of Christ holding open a book, and a picture of the Holy Trinity sat around a table in muted, yet somehow glowing and vibrant, shades of blue and gold. She'd kneel down, read a passage from the Gospel, then simply sit in silence till the hour was up. She'd conclude by saying the Our Father, or something similar, in Latin. These morning sessions were always hard work for me to get myself to, but whenever I did make it – two or three times in total, I think – they always felt exceptionally worthwhile, and the sense of peace and stillness stayed with me for the rest of the day. 'This is the way to go,' I thought. 'This is the future.'

I had a sense, however, that Vivi was a lot sadder on some deep level than she'd been before. Not that she was moping around or anything, more that it seemed there was something on her mind. I thought it might be connected with boys (or men in her case), though I'd never known her have a boyfriend ever. There were always guys who liked her, though, and I know that caused her difficulties. She had been doing a lot of one-on-one work too – helping people with their problems, including, believe it or not, Mandy Mitten, who had done really well since school and was now a trainee vet. Obviously, she still had a few of her million and one problems left though. It kind of cheered me to know that not all that much, with some people at least, had really changed.

Except the weather. The grey was gone. Yay! Banished to the Kingdom of Greyness. Yesterday, and the day before, were gorgeous (if totally brassic) days of low, blinding sun and razor-sharp frost. There's no better place to be on such days, in my book, than the Walker Art Gallery café. The sun shines through the brown-framed doors, giving you the illusion that it's the sun warming you up, rather than the heating, already groaning and creaking and cranked up to the max. Early in the morning it's so nice and quiet, with just a few staff pottering about, ideal really, either for sitting on your own and chilling or having a serious chat. I couldn't have thought of a better venue and was delighted Vivi had chosen it. It was my last full day, and I sensed something stirring in her. A revelation of some kind, I hoped.

I had a latté. Vivi had a mint tea. We sat on one of the white rectangular tables near the middle of the café, just to the left of the statue in the middle – a man in Greek or Roman soldier's costume, sword in hand and striding forward, poised to make a stand and intervene in the cause of right.

'Are you sure you're okay, Vivi?' I began. 'In yourself, I mean. You've seemed a bit down. A bit preoccupied. Are you sad about Ma?'

Vivi stirred the big green leaves in her tea and smiled. She was pale and wan. Her eyes looked tired. Two gallery staff in blue shirts stood above, leaning on the balcony of the 'o' shaped 'polo hole' (as Gina called it) upstairs. They were talking about football – something to do with Liverpool and Man United. Radios crackled.

'Of course I'm sad, Jules. You are too. Maybe you don't realise it yet, but you are. I'm sad for Mum, but I'm glad as well, because she's at peace now and is, I believe, if not yet with God then certainly on her way. She had a hard life and did her best. He will be a merciful judge.'

'Yes, that's true,' I said. 'It's not sunk in yet. I'll know about it when it does, I guess.'

'Me too. We're both in the same boat.'

She sipped her tea. 'Ow. Hot.' She blew her cheeks in and out for a second or two, face glowing red like a furnace.'

'Naturally,' she continued, 'I look at myself in all this. I'm conscious of my sin, Julie, both with regards to how I've looked after Mum, or failed to do that, and also with how I've looked after you, or, again, failed to look after you. You're right to sense I've been a bit down. I've got a lot on my mind. I feel like I've failed on both counts. It's why I had my hair cut, I reckon. Subconsciously anyway. A symbolic penance.'

I was really upset about that. That wasn't what I wanted to hear. 'Oh, Vivi, Vivi. Please don't be hard on yourself. It's me who's the silly one. It's me who should've listened to you. I'm listening now, Vivi. Can't you see? Can't you hear? I'm changing my life. I want to be good. I want to be holy. I want to be like you.'

'If you were like me,' said Vivi, 'you'd be a liar and a scoundrel.'

'No. Vivi. Please.'

She grabbed my lapels and pulled me to her. I glanced above. The gallery staff had gone. There was no-one else around. Even the café guy had vanished. It was probably just as well. Vivi spoke in a whisper, but I'd never felt such power and force in a whisper before.

'You want to hear a confession, don't you? A revelation. I know you like the back of my hand, Jules. You love a good drama. You think you've outgrown it but it'll never go away. It's who you are. It's your *charism* – what God called you to be. Now, listen up, how's this for a bit of drama? I didn't want you to go to Manchester because I didn't want you to go through the confusion and weirdness that I did. I do want you to go back, however, and see things out, because I feel we both owe a debt to Ambrosius Carlisle.'

'Y-y-y-ou, Vivi? How? Wh-wh-why?'

'Because I was a student of his. Years ago. Around the time Dad started telling you stories.'

'Whaaaat?'

'Remember the corner of Rodney and Leece?'

I shook her off and slammed my latté down. 'Oh, Jesus Christ, Vivi.' Milky-white foam frothed over the glass.

'Julie, please.'

'Don't "please" me, for fuck's sake. I *knew* it was you. I *knew* it was you. And yet you said it wasn't. That night in my room. I asked you and you said it wasn't. You said I was over-imagining, a "prisoner of fantasy," or something. Fucking Hell. Do you realise how much that's fucked me up all through my life?'

I sat back, folded my arms, stamped my foot and put on a stroppy face, pouting like a sulky French actress. It was all for show though. Secretly I was glad. I had been proved right. Vivi's words backed me up. I mean, I'd *known* it was her. I'd seen her. It was unmistakeably her. No hyper-imaginistic teenager could magic up such a spectacular apparition. Vivi's confession gave me a boost. It felt like 'one-nil' to my worldview, and it was funny, I reflected, how delighted I was for my old 'mythic' way of seeing things, after spending the last fortnight dissing it and 'moving on' and all that blah.

Vivi let things settle. My anger, such as it was, quickly passed. She sipped her tea. Drinkable now. A fella of about forty-odd in a blue coat and grey scarf that covered half his face sat two tables to our right with exactly the same brew as Vivi. I wondered, absent-mindedly, if he was one of Jacqueline's 'spies'.

Vivi picked up the thread. 'I apologise, Julie. I should have been honest with you, but because you'd been having such a bad time and had bit that girl at school…'

'Oh, why're you reminding me of that?'

'Because it was serious, Jules. You were out of control. Dad papered over the cracks, but his stories gave you the most terrible nightmares.'

'They didn't.'

'They did. Don't try to rewrite history. You're always trying to rewrite history.'

'I had *one* nightmare, then *you* had the cheek to tell me a load of porkies before reading from the Bible. Honestly, Vivi. What are you like?'

'I lied, and I'm sorry. But I lied for the right reasons. If you had known what was going on, it would have sent you over the edge.'

'Why, what *was* going on?'

'Oh nothing,' Vivi said in a softer tone. 'Nothing dubious, I mean. All we ever did, Carlisle and I, was work on Shakespeare's Roman plays: *Julius Caesar, Antony and Cleopatra, Corialanus*; *Cymbeline* as well, I think. He had just come back from France at the time. He was living in Manchester and wanted to start an artistic community. This was before Constantine's Chambers, you see. I don't know if there was anyone else he was working with. It was always just me and him in this upper room he hired out.'

'Just you and him? Sounds a bit ropy.'

'I was nineteen, Julie. I'd just started university. All the way up in Edinburgh. I was big enough to look after myself. But it was nothing like that at all. Honestly, it wasn't. Carlisle's a monk. A genuine, *bona-fide* monk. He treats his vocation with the high seriousness. He became a Chlorian in France, about ten years ago. And that's what made me wary of him. His *Chlorianness*, if that makes sense. He could have been a Carmelite, a Benedictine, a Cistercian, a Trappist. Anything. But no, he had to become a Chlorian, the most right-wing and reactionary of all the orders, with dangerous occult leanings to boot.'

'What do you mean? I don't understand.'

I was lying. I understood full well.

'Look, Julie, you've seen it yourself. He's a fantastic teacher. Inspirational. I loved that side of it. I came back from Edinburgh, six Thursdays in a row, just to be with him. No-one brings Shakespeare alive like he does. It's a tragedy, an absolute tragedy, that because he's a bit eccentric and holds certain political views, that universities and mainstream media don't want to touch him.'

'What went wrong then?'

'Well, in the fourth week he wanted me to act out some dialogue he'd written himself about the Holy Grail being discovered in a Nazi-occupied Britain.'

'Ah, that sounds familiar.'

'I had to walk from one end of the room to the other with this chalice in my hands, say a few lines, then drink from it, put it down, and stand in the window for a minute. I just thought it totally blasphemous, a parody of the Last Supper. That's what I told him. He said he wouldn't do it again, but he kept trying to sneak it back in, so in the end I stopped coming.'

'Was he angry?'

'No, I don't think so.'

'What about you? Do you regret it?'

'No. Only that I didn't tell you at the time and didn't tell you again this summer. Seeing as you were so determined to go, I thought it best to let it all lie. It wouldn't have made any difference if you'd known. That's what I thought. I'm a bit disappointed in Mr. Martin though. He's Carlisle's most devoted disciple, you know. He snared me years ago, now he's snared you. The least he could've done is told me he was going to approach you. I don't think he knew what a bad time you'd had before you went to St. Mark's though.'

'Oh yes he did. I told him.'

'Well, there you go then. Silly old Sea Dog.'

'But what about you? Did you enjoy it? The experience, I mean.'

'Yes, of course. I just wish he'd kept to Shakespeare. Still, it gave me a few ideas about retreat giving and spiritual direction, though I'm thinking along different lines now.'

The last bit of her answer passed me by. 'What about Dad?' I asked. 'Where did you stay? How did you keep it a secret?'

'I didn't. Dad was in on it. He smuggled me in after midnight and spirited me back to Lime Street next day. He sorted my train tickets too. Neither Mum nor yourself had any idea. "Our secret". That's what he called it. '

'Whaaaat?'

'He first met Carlisle at the station, he said. On the forecourt. A routine question about train times apparently. Somehow it blossomed – if that's the right word – into a deep mutual appreciation. Dad was obsessed with Carlisle. He thought he was the best. He was desperate for me to work with him. He was so disappointed when I said I was stopping.'

'I don't understand. How close did they get? Did Dad work with him in any way?'

'Well, I don't really know. Dad stopped confiding in me after that. I'd already rejected his stories too, don't forget. I think he'd had enough of me, and that's when he turned his attention to you. It's interesting though, the way things have worked out. Mr. Martin told me once that Carlisle wanted Dad as his bard, much as he now wants you as his bard.'

Vivi finished her tea and leant close in. 'Here's the thing, Jules. Dad was about to leave home and go and live with Carlisle the year Constantine's Chambers was set up. That was the year he died. Suddenly and mysteriously.'

'Mysteriously? Whattya mean?' I was aghast. I looked around the café, like someone might be lining me up with a gun hidden in a bunch of flowers. A couple of old dears – 'Darby and Joan' types – were sitting between us and the doors now. The bloke in the coat and scarf was still drinking his tea, reading (or pretending to read) The Telegraph.

'Oh well,' said Vivi, coyly. 'I'm sure it *was* just a heart attack. A congenital heart defect. But none of us saw it happen, you know. You were at school, I was upstairs and Ma was nattering out the front. It was Cecylia who found him.'

'Cecylia?'

'The lodger.'

'Ah yeah. Adam and Cecylia.'

'She said she saw someone climbing over the wall in the yard.'

'Who?'

'A man in a balaclava.'

'No.'

'Yes.'

'Who was he?'

'A robber maybe. Or an enemy of Carlisle's. He'a got one or two. Either that or…'

'Or what?'

'Mrs. Hunt's husband,' Vivi blurted, 'or a hit-man hired by him.'

'Whaaaat?'

Vivi looked away – pale, speechless, struggling for breath.

'Mrs. Hunt? Oh my God, Vivi. Oh my God. You're joking me. Tell me you're joking. You're fuckin' jesting me.'
She held my hand in hers. 'I'm not, Jules, my love. I wish I was. I wish to God I was.'

'W-w-w-w-what's it all about? What's Mrs. H-hunt got to do with it?'

It was a pointless question. I knew the answer already. I'd always known the answer.

'Dad had a liaison with her, for about a year or so, around the time you had your troubles.'

I squeezed her hand as tight as I could and put my left hand up to my eyes to catch the tears. And that was all I could do. I dissolved into a big fucking mess, elbows slammed down on the table, coffee spilling all over the place, sobbing and mewling and gasping and heaving like the heart, soul, core and guts of my world had been ripped out and thrown to the dogs. 'Dad, Dad, Dad.' Everything else Vivi had told me I could handle, and even see as a bit of a giggle, but this, no, oh God no. I remembered Vivi's prayer that morning: 'Lord Jesus Christ, Son of God, have mercy on me, a sinner.' And I said it over and over again in my heart, clinging to it, hugging it tight, and the 'me', the 'sinner', was everyone – everyone tied up in this whole sorry mess: Dad, Ma, Vivi, me, Caesar, Mr.

Martin, Dr. Tenby, Mrs. Hunt, Mrs. Hunt's husband, Jacqueline, Romulus, Claire, Lolek, Glinka, Adam, Cecylia, Jim, Camilla, Philip, Jean-Luc and Claire.

'Lord Jesus Christ, Son of God, have mercy on me, a sinner.'

XIX

'Why, for Christ's sake?' I asked the next morning, fierce frost and shrimming cold nipping and tugging our faces. We walked along Renshaw Street, heading for the station and a return (for me) to Constantine's Chambers. Vivi wore a dark blue ski-hat that covered her hair and made the most of her super-fine, super-chiselled cheekbones. She held my sports bag in her left hand.

'Here,' she said, diving into the pocket of her black winter jacket with her right. 'I've written you a letter. It'll say more there than I can put into words.'

'Alright, Vivi, thanks.'

I took the letter. I felt a little *frisson* when I saw my name in her handwriting on the envelope: *Julie*.

Then I saw something lying on the pavement that lightened my mood – a long curvy twig with other smaller twigs branching off from it, and just the tiniest hint of yellowed-out leaves on the branches. I picked it up and held it in front of my face. 'What play's this, Vivi?'

She laughed and clapped her gloved hands. 'Oh, Julie, you *are* funny,' she said. 'I have absolutely no idea.'

'*Macbeth*,' I said triumphantly, quoting:

'Be lion-mettled, proud, and take no care

Who chafes, who frets, or where conspirers are.

Macbeth shall never vanquished be until

Great Birnam Wood to high Dunsinane Hill

Shall come against him.

Then continuing with:

As I did stand my watch upon the hill

I looked toward Birnam, and anon, methought,

The wood began to move.'

Vivi was impressed. 'I should have got that, shouldn't I? You're an English soldier pretending to be a tree.'

We laughed and swept through the concourse.

'1016, Platform Four,' I said.

'I'll see you off.'

'You've not got a ticket.'

'Doesn't matter. No-one looks.'

Vivi was right. No-one did. The men at the barrier were discussing a manager called 'Cheeseman' who had annoyed them. They smiled at us both though.

It was nearly time. 'Here y'are, Vivi.' I pulled out the picture of Constantius and the silver-haired woman. 'Take this,' I said, theatrically but sincerely, 'as a token of my love, and the bond that exists between us. Yesterday, today and always.' And then, as she hugged and kissed me: 'There's one in every room, so I'm sure he's a job-lot of 'em somewhere. He won't miss one.'

Vivi smiled and studied the painting. 'It's beautiful, Jules,' was what she said.'Just like an icon. Just like you.'

And she held me in her arms again.

****

Once on board, I regretted not buying a coffee, but I did have a bottle of Oasis in my bag, so I opened it up and guzzled it down as I undid Vivi's envelope. The train was quiet. There was no-one next to me, so I stretched out my legs to the right and started to read:

My Dearest Julie,

Thank you so much for allowing me to unburden myself yesterday. It was a hard conversation, I know, but I suspect that this morning (I'm up bright and early, you see, writing this before morning prayer) we will both feel clearer and happier in our hearts, minds and souls.

I would like, if possible please, for you not to judge our poor father too harshly. We both benefited greatly from the upbringing he gave us. Our young lives, generally speaking, were happy and stable. We never felt short of anything, least of all love and affection. I know as little as you regarding his family background. I gather, however, that his father only physical work and did not encourage his imaginative capabilities. Dad came to England hoping to find his calling as a writer, but lacked not only connections and contacts but also the discipline, it seems, to complete a novel or collection of short stories. In any case, writing was far from his forté, as you know better than most. Spoken word was where he came into his own, as Ambrosius Carlisle was very swift to recognise.

Dad and Carlisle were kindred spirits, I think, in that they both felt they could find no outlet in society for their intellect and creativity. Carlisle, who is exceptionally well-educated, has built up his own alternative establishment, but has compromised himself dreadfully in muddying the waters between politics, drama, religion and mythology. There is an enormous psychological projection taking place here, I believe. Dad, on the other hand, for all his bravado and 'bardic' persona, just wanted someone to believe in him and take his imagination seriously. There was a vacuum in his life, and Carlisle filled it. This gave him a burst of creative energy that spilled over into his affair with Mrs. Hunt and soured a marriage that had already been struggling (though they kept it well hidden in the main) due to Mum's irritation with his delusions of grandeur and the gap between his mythic visions and their day to day lives. I have suggested as well that it might have played a contributory role in the circumstances surrounding his premature death.

All this feels quite heavy stuff at times, doesn't it, Julie? I have been meditating on these matters for a long time, and have felt sometimes a little like Antigone, or any of the heroes and heroines of Greek tragedy, condemned to pay for misdemeanours committed by previous generations. I have concluded (and this is my fourth and final revelation!) that the best step for me in the future is the most radical one imaginable. I have, over the past year, been paying frequent visits to the Carmelite Priory at Quidenham, Norfolk, and I hope to enter as a Postulant (that's the very first stage, by the way, so still, an awfully long way to go) in September next year, after my MA is completed.

Quidenham is inspired by the spiritual vision and way of life outlined for us by Saint Teresa of Avila. Contemplative prayer is at the centre of community life, and this is where I feel God is calling me to live out my own vocation, wrestling, like Jacob at the Jabbok, with my own depth of sin and the world's weight of sin, until both the world and myself are blessed and given new names. I have been tremendously impressed with Carmelite spirituality, Julie. It radiates humility and simplicity, while possessing a profound understanding of the human condition. Wherever Carmelites are found, they speak to the world of God and spiritual realities. The sisters at Quidenham value the companionship of Jesus above all other things. They are aware of all the sin and suffering, sadness and despair throughout the world, as am I, and know that only Jesus has the answer. They want everyone to feel the peace, love and happiness Christ longs to give, so they choose on behalf of their fellow men and women to live out with him, every day and every night, the mystery of His life and death, dedicating themselves solely to Him.

My dear Julie, I know that this will come as yet another shock, but please do not despair just because we may have to see each other less in the physical world. Rejoice, rather, that God has given me the grace to hear and respond to his call in the way that suits best my character and personality.

I pray, dear Julie, that your last week at Constantine's Chambers may pass without incident and that Ambrosius and Jacqueline can perhaps sit down and discuss their differences, which, in the last analysis, may be more apparent than real.

I am returning to London for a few days now. I look forward to seeing you on the 22nd and spending Christmas and New Year together for the last time in the old house.

Love and blessings,

V x

I looked up. The train was shooting past the skyscraper that swallowed up half the sky on my last trip. I was amazed. Flabberghasted. I'd arrived already. I must have spent the whole journey reading Vivi's letter, over and over again until I knew it by heart.

Constantine's Chambers was all a-bustle when I got back. A white glazier's van was parked on the drive. 'M20 Glass,' said the orange script. Men in blue overalls shuffled in and out, ferrying sheets of glass.

'What's going on?' I said to Jim, who was standing in the hallway, giving directions.

He rattled off his reply like I hadn't been away at all and that nothing of importance (such as my mother dying) had happened in my life. 'Caesar was demonstrating another of his *contretemps* with weapons in Shakespeare. This time a spear in *Timon*. He used a cue from the billiard room' (I didn't even know we had a billiard room) 'but lost control of it. Straight through the window. Whole thing needs replacing.'

'Where?'

'Dining room.'

'Wow, I've missed a bit of action then.'

'I'll say.'

Then he was off; sprinting away to inspect the repairs. 'Well, well,' I reflected. 'I've not made much of an impact there. Might as well be invisible.'

Everyone else was really nice to me though. 'Sorry about your Mum, Julie,' said some. 'Great to have you back,' said others. Even miserablists such as Philip and Camilla seemed genuinely delighted to see me. I could tell that they really, sincerely wished me well. As did Jacqueline when I met her on the stairs. I had been thinking, on the bus ride down, about what she had said about her dad being an economic forecaster.

'Did you ever know a chap called Ronald Tenby?' I asked on the off-chance. 'Old guy. Historian. White hair, white beard.' Jacqueline nodded, carried on down, then turned her head and smiled. She was all in black – jumper, skirt, leggings and shoes – and looked exceedingly chic. She raised her eyebrows. 'I know him very well,' she said. 'He was a frequent visitor at one time. He's taught me a lot. No doubt about that.' Then she turned and continued on her way.

I wanted to find Caesar to tell him what I'd decided, but he was with a school group in the Drama Space and the door was closed. I could hear the kids repeating – sharply, rhythmically, with bounce and verve – the opening line of *Richard II*: 'Old John of Gaunt, time-honoured Lancaster,' over and over again. Their bright voices merged in my mind with the mid-winter sun, and I was glad to be back.

I popped out for a bite (food, that is) to Expo with Claire and had a cheeky glass of Sambuca on the side. Claire didn't drink, as she was working there straight after. But I took my time, reading the papers, then going for a walk by the river, and then, when it was dark, strolling through the frost-tinged backstreets for a while until 'dinner' was safely past. I'd had enough of people by now, you see, no matter how lovely they'd been. I needed a bit of 'Julie time.'

Back in my room, I realised I still had the red bandana on. 'It may as well stay there,' I thought, 'until the end of the day.' I took off my jumper and jeans and put on a tunic instead – one I'd not worn before – the white one with the purple diamond on the front. I slipped on my silver-buckled shoes and tied my tunic with the red belt.

The room felt warm and cosy. I still had Jacqueline and Dr. Tenby on my mind. I wondered, out of the blue, if I should have a go at writing a spy story. It'd be something different. Away from the usual run of myths and legends. Might even make me a bit of money.

I got my jotter out and was ready to sit down at the desk when I heard a noise outside. I pulled back the curtain and had a sly peek. I gasped and put my hand to my mouth. About twenty black-clad, balaclava wearing figures were marching along the street in the form of a 'V', their leader at the tip and the others fanning out behind. I closed the curtains again, crouched down and carried on peeping through the gap in the middle. They were too close for comfort now, the leader right front of Constantine's Chambers, in fact. He raised his right hand and the formation halted. One or two of them got down on all fours and started to crawl towards the house.

It could, of course, have been some kind of theatrical game sponsored by Jim or Caesar himself maybe. But I doubted it. There was something far too intent in the way these guys were going about their business. The phrase, 'citizen's arrest', came back to my mind, and I understood, there and then, that it had been a total red herring.

This was it. This was the arrest. Right here, right now. Pre-planned for ages. Catching everyone by surprise. I felt frightened and sick. My stomach ached. But even as I panicked I recognised, once and for all, which side my bread was buttered on. I could think only of Ceasar and the Grail. I had to find Caesar and tell him. I had to rescue the Grail. Those two tasks mattered more than anything else, cutting through all my 'fresh starts' and 'blank slates' like shears through jelly. I jumped up, yet again dragging down my sports bag, then ran from the room, just as I was, in my tunic, headband and shoes. Caesar's chamber was dark and empty. Shit. Only one thing to do. Get Lolek to open up.

'The key, Lolek. The key.'

'But, Miss Julie...'

KERPOW...

Down in the chapel, as I said at the start, Caesar stopped me in my tracks. He looked so calm, so composed and centred, that it seemed incredible that anything could happen without his say-so. Yet there they were. I could hear them upstairs. Hammering at the doors.

'Take the Grail and its Hallows, *Mith* Carlton. Bury them away for a season in some secret place. I will come again for them at the consummation of the age, which now lies nigh at hand. Go, Miss Carlton, my bard, and God speed your holy quest.'

But before I could go I had to find a way of stuffing everything into the bag. It was impossible. The spear, obviously, wouldn't go in at all; the sword would only go half in; the stone weighed a ton; and the chalice rolled around and banged against the stone so much that I was sure it'd be half-destroyed before I even got out of the garden.

Eventually though, the task was completed. I stood before Caesar. The altar and its flickering candles stood gold and white behind his back. I couldn't see the book. Where was the book?

'I have the book, my child,' said Caesar, reading my mind. 'I need to go on writing it, for the duration of my exile – this book of dreams and prophecies – this book of past, present and future.'

There were so many things I wanted to say to him; so many things I needed to say – about the book, about my life, about the world and Constantine's Chambers and everything happening above and outside. Yet all I could manage was: 'I was going to write a spy story before, Caesar. Before I saw them coming, I mean. I was going to give up on myths and legends.'

Caesar smiled and held out his hand. I shook it. His face was boyish and playful. 'You'll never do that, Miss Carlton. You are incapable. It is not who you are. Be who you are. That is the best and only advice that I can give. Now go, and may the ancient, eternal light – Roma Principia – be with you always.'

I bowed, turned and ran up the straight stone stairs, finding it even harder than last time with Claire. It isn't easy running up stairs, as I say, and it's a whole lot harder when you've got a bag of Medieval antiques in one arm and a big bronze spear in the other.

They were already in. Shitsticks. 'Kill him if you see him,' boomed a male voice from the direction of the studio. 'Don't take any chances. He's a dangerous fucker.'

Something was burning. Liquid oozed along the dining room floor. No time to lose. I put down my bag, picked up a chair and launched it against the dining room window that had only that very day been put on. SHATTER, SMASH, SHATTER. Now I'd a hole I could get through. A blast of cold air nearly floored me before I'd even got going. It was crazily cold outside. Beyond brassic. I ran through the garden, past the outhouse, then chucked the bag, as best I could, on top of the garage. I hauled myself up, crawled along for a bit, then readied myself to jump down onto the street. Then I saw something that really upset me – Lolek curled up in a ball on the pavement, with two balaclava'd goons booting him again and again him in the body and head. 'Fascist twat,' one of them grunted. I sprang down, swung the spear and poleaxed the speaker with its shaft. Down he went like a sack of spuds, but that was all I could do. I had to leave Lolek to it, much as I hated to, because more of the knobheads were pouring down the street now, not in formation anymore, but running right at me like they were desperate to grab me. 'That's her,' they shouted. 'Get her.' 'Scouse bitch,' 'Psycho,' 'Fuckin' Dracula,' and so on.

I darted left and ran. The rooftops, chimneys and telegraph wires looked beautiful in the icy night. Lights switched on in houses. A brown-haired toddler in Man City pyjamas watched me run from a living room window. At the end of the road a junction. Balaclavas coming from the right. Go left, Julie. Straight on. Get to the village. Get to Expo and Claire. They'll melt away there. People in Didsbury won't stand for balaclavas. It'll them that'll be arrested, not me.

I came to the area Claire called 'toy town'. No pretend townhouses here, just basic, brown brick affairs, purpose-built gaffs for old folks, I think. I could see the village now, thirty metres or so ahead. Nearly there. Nearly there. And then, for the first time, I saw them coming at me from in front as well.

Fuckery.

There's a little street that goes nowhere, just before 'toy town' begins, with a bit of waste ground behind it and a mesh-like gate in front. I was out on my feet. I could run no more. Time to stand or fall. I pulled out the sword, then dropped the bag to the ground. I held it up with my right hand. Starlight glinted on steel. I held up the spear with my left. The bronze pulsed and throbbed, the tip an angry, bloody, scarlet dart.

The pack drew back. 'Cum 'ead,' I shouted ... 'Come and get 'em if you dare.'

They fell back and stood in a semi-circle, five metres off or so, muttering and cursing uneasily. 'Winner,' I thought. But then a tall figure in black broke through the ranks. Jacqueline ripped off her balaclava and stood in front of me, eyes cold and hostile. I stared back at her. A gigantic explosion rent and split the freezing air. 'It's fuckin' gone up,' someone said, but neither of us blinked. None of that mattered anymore: Ceasar, Constantine's Chambers, the Grail. Just the two of us now.

'You promised me a fight,' she said.

'I did.'

'Make the most of it then. It'll be your last.'

A super-long leg telescoped up at the speed of light, sending the sword flying. Then she was on me, wrenching the spear from my grasp, and then we were down on the floor, wrestling and grappling like crazy. I knew straightaway she wanted me dead, either by strangling me or bouncing my head up and down on the concrete. I had a job on my hands, make no mistake. Jacqueline was big and strong and tough, all arms and legs and intense, electric, flame-like energy. It was like riding a tiger. I had my work cut out just to cling on. It all seemed a very long way from scrabbling around on the Royal Exchange floor with Bella Chung.

Then, little by little, I began to get used to her rhythms and thrusts and started to launch a counter or two of my own. I was desperate to get a bite in. Either that or claw out her eyes. That was my other tactic. I spotted the sword lying on the ground, behind me and to my left. 'That'll change the dynamic,' I thought. I reached first with my left hand, then two things struck me at once: first that the sword was no longer there, and second that the pressure of Jacqueline's body and hands no longer oppressed me. She'd let go and was kneeling on the ground to my right, her face cut and red and bruised, brown hair strewn all over her face. But her eyes were rapt. Shining and bright. No hostility now. She scrambled to her feet. As did I. Slowly. Painfully. I followed the direction of her eyes with mine, then saw what she saw, the most beautiful, astonishing, incredible sight – an angel hovering in the air, three feet off the ground, with bright white hair and swishing robes of maroon-tinged silver. His right hand held the sword aloft, his left hand held the spear, and his gaze (his eyes were wide and brown, like the eyes of Christ in Vivi's icon) pierced my soul and blew a cleansing wind through all the nooks and crannies of my being. He knew my secrets. My inmost parts. My name, my calling, my vocation. In a moment he would give me my new name – my true name – the one, I realised now, that I had spent my whole life wrestling night and day with him to learn.

Jacqueline took my left hand in hers, squeezed it and squeezed again when I squeezed it back. Then came the sound of sirens. The angel faded into the stars and frost. 'I've got them,

Jackie,' hollered a familiar voice. 'I've got them all,' Hand in hand we turned around and faced the crowd. Romulus Charles, also dressed in black, but without a balaclava, held the sword and spear together in his right hand and my sports bag in his left. 'You can let the Scouser go. They'll nick her as soon as they see her anyway.'

I bowed and shook my head. How dare he trample on our miracle like that? Our special, sacred moment. Our holy vision.

Jacqueline tried to hold me back, but there was no holding me. None at all. I was off like a shot, flinging myself at the loser, punching, kicking, spitting, and yes, biting, again and again and again, till he cried out in pain, the soft twat. But then, somehow, the tables were turned, and it was me skriking and crying. I had more and more people on top of me, swarming me, jumping me, crushing me under the weight of their boots and bodies and fists. I heard Jacqueline's voice. 'No, let her go.' But it was too late. I was hurled into a van or a waggon. Inside was dark, but outside all I could hear was one explosion after the other, then sirens, then alarms, then people shouting and screaming, until the world grew dim around me and I found myself alone in this room and lying on this bed.

XX

So, what's going to happen now? My story's done and dusted. I'm still in pain and it's still all dark.

Then, just like that, it's not. I see light peeping under the door and around the sides, stealing stealthily into the room. Footsteps outside. I try to sit up, but my stomach's giving me grief, so I lie back down.

The door opens and three people enter the room. I recognise two of them immediately – Dr. Tenby and Mr. Martin. Mr. Martin stands to the right and Dr. Tenby to the left. In the centre stands a woman with a lamp. The lamp is so bright that I can't see her face. All three wear short-sleeved tunics: Mr. Martin in red, with a yellow lightning flash on the front; Dr. Tenby in a pale blue creation with a silver star in the middle; and the third, central person in a black tunic with an equal-armed cross in the middle.

Mr. Martin speaks first, his face as red as his tunic. 'Miss Carlton's friends deserve to see her, Commandant. Miss Calcanti, Mr. Carter and Miss Falconer have proved loyal and true over so many years. And in any case, this girl should not be left lying here like this. She will die from her wounds.'

The middle person speaks, and I'm glad, once I've heard her, that I can't see her face. Her voice belongs to Mrs. Hunt. 'She may well die from her wounds,' it says, 'and that is to be regretted. It needs to be said, however, that this girl has brought her plight entirely upon herself. A most violent girl, gentlemen, with a penchant for biting and spitting – foul-mouthed, aggressive, confused and unable to function in society. If she does survive, she will need years of rehabilitation. She will need to be kept from society too, such as it is. Do not look at her so much, Mr. Martin. It will inflame her and make her mad.'

At this Mr. Martin gets very cross, pointing to the ceiling as he passionately defends me. 'What disgraceful nonsense. This girl is one of the choice and master spirits of the age. She is an independent, creative thinker, a genuine, *bona fide* free spirit. The world needs its Julie Carlton's, if it is ever to solve the problems that have brought it to such ruin. It needs that vision and fire. Without vision, the people perish.'

Dr. Tenby holds his left arm out, palm down, on the other side of the lantern. 'David, David. Calm yourself, please. Miss Carlton will live, I am sure. She is a tough, nuggety competitor. But by encouraging her *vis-a-vis* Constantine's Chambers, David, you have played a contributory role, whether you like it or not, in her downfall. This kid thinks she can walk through walls. Well, she can't. Nor can I. Nor can you. As much as we long for spiritual freedom and emancipation from external laws, we cannot be entirely freed from the outer world and its restrictions without spiralling down into chaos.' He shakes his woolly head. 'Walking through walls,' he concludes, 'is for the angels alone.'

Mr. Martin stamps his foot and gives a little pout. I giggle. It's funny. 'Well, that's just typical of you, isn't it Roland? Let's call a spade a spade, eh? You're an American spy, aren't you? I don't know why you don't admit it. Everyone knows you're on the CIA payroll.'

Dr. Tenby shrugs. 'Preserving order is what I am all about, David. I see no shame in that. I am a realist, and realism, in my view, should not be a dirty word. My whole *oeuvre* has been dedicated to confining political, spiritual and cultural instability to the margins of society. I break laws where required, I'll have you know. I am not afraid of ruthless action in defence of stabilty. I am a historian, David. I have learnt the value and worth of the 'balance of power.' He coughs. 'Russell Paul, on the other hand ....'

'Oh how many times do I have to tell you?' says Mr. Martin. 'His name is Ambrosius Carlisle.'

'No,' I shout, sitting up despite the pain. 'His name's not Russell Paul, nor Ambrosius Carlisle. His name's Augustus Ceasar. Augustus Ceasar, do you hear?'

They don't hear me though. They can't. That's the distressing thing. No matter how much I shout and bawl, they can't hear a word I say. They don't seem to see me properly either. It's like I'm lying down asleep, when I'm not asleep at all. I'm wide awake and talking at the top of my voice, but no-one can hear me. I've got straps on the bed as well, I notice, hemming me in, holding me down, like I'm a nut-job or something. It really upsets me. I start to cry, and forget they're there. They go out of the room and I'm left on my own again, in a room beginning at last to turn grey. I close my eyes and let go of it all, no longer fussing and striving to have a vocation or a calling as a storyteller or a bard or anything. I let go and release – down, down and down again – crashing through squares and walls of greyness – depth after depth, layer after layer – down, down and down again – until I've gone so far down that I can't go any more down – going up, up and up now – until I'm out of the grey and into the white, or onto the white – white rocks, to be precise – with wind and sea and sky around me. It is morning. Cool and frseh. Tall, noble figures surround me in a ring. My blue mantle ripples in the wind. I loosen my headband, strum my harp and settle into my song:

Now comes the hour foretold, a god-gift bringing a wonder sight.
Is it a star new-born and splendid, up-springing out of night?
Is it a wave from the Fountain of Beauty, up-flinging Foam of
delight?
Is it a glorious immortal bird, winging hither its flight?

It is a wave, high-crested, melodious, triumphant, breaking in light.
It is a star, rose-hearted and joyous, a splendour risen from night.
It is flame from the world of the gods, and love runs before it,
A quenchless delight.

Let the wave break, let the star rise, let the flame leap.
Ours, if our hearts are wise, to take, cherish and keep.

At last, at last, at last. The first story. The goddess come to meet me. Dad's voice ringing in my ear again. His hand holding mine. One more time around the streets and squares of Liverpool 8…

'Come,' says Bridget. 'I am going to wrap my blue mantle around the Earth, because the Earth has dreamed and sang of beauty.'

'I will forge a place for it,' said Midyir. 'I will bring fire to the monsters.'

'I will come too,' said the Dagda.

'And I,' said Ogma the Wise, Splendour of the Sun.

'And I,' said Nuada, Wielder of the White Light.

'And I,' said Gobniu the Wonder Smith.

'Fare forward, voyagers,' said Angus Og. 'Fair forward. I would go myself if only you had the Sword of Light.'

'We will take the Sword of Light,' said Bridget, 'and the Cauldron of Plenty, and the Spear of Victory, and the Stone of Destiny.'

'It is nobly said,' cried all the Shining Ones. 'We will take the Four Jewels.'

So, Ogma brought the Sword of Light from Findrias, the cloud-bright city at the world's Eastern gate; Nuada brought the Spear of Victory from Gorias, the flame-bright city standing in the Southern Quarter; the Dagda brought the Cauldron of Plenty from Murias, the city of the West, the city of flowing waters; and Midyir brought the Stone of Destiny from Falias the city built high into the mountains of the North, the great city of iron.'

Then the Shining Ones set forth. They fell like a shower of stars till they arrived at the blackness ringing the earth, and, looking down, saw below them the horned and savage heads of men and women bellowing and roaring in the heart of chaos, and the adamantine chains of the lost souls and prisoners, those who have failed, those who have lost their way, those who have missed their calling, those who have been unable to find an outlet.'

I, Julie, am Bridget now, older and younger than the world itself. My harp has turned into a hoop, a golden hoop, alive with gemstones and subtle fire. I am looking for Geraldine. I find her crouching down, bound in chains. I touch the iron with my hoop, the chains creak, break, crack and fall away. Geraldine arises, and I am Geraldine now as well. Geraldine, Bridget and Julie.

My hoop has gone. I know not where or how. But I'm not sad. Not this time. It has played its part and played it well. I walk the length of a long underground corridor until I come to a flight of straight stone steps. At the top of is a door. I open it, walk through, and there I am back home again, in the great sweeping circle of the Catholic Cathedral. Long, curvy benches fan out and around from the High Altar in the middle. Slim, blue, vertical stained-glass strips line the circle, as blue as the Sea of Galilee in my picture-book Bible. If you sit there long enough, you know, you'll see flashes of red, like salamanders or Hebrew letters, springing to life on the blue, while high on the walls the tapestries flow and stream around: Our Lady of Liverpool, Christ holding open the Gospel, flakes of fire falling upon the Apostles heads, and so many more.

There's a man standing with his back to me at the altar dressed in white with a purple sash arrowing down from his right shoulder. I climb the altar steps and he turns to face me. He has white hair and a white beard. Or that's what I see at first. Then golden hair and golden beard. In his hands he holds a scroll. 'My name,' he says, 'is Melchizedek. I am old and young at once, standing at the end of the world and its beginning, the servant, priest and scribe of the Most High God.' He holds out the scroll. 'Write, Julie,' he says.

'But Sir, I have no pen.'

'Write,' he says. 'Write, write, write. Become what thou art.'

I take the scroll. It's warm to my touch. 'Surely,' I think, 'this can only mean one thing …'

XXI

The consummation of the age. Nothing less than that. The ending of this silly, stupid world. Yay!

But is it really all that silly? Isn't it me in reality, who's been the silly, stupid one, not the beaten down, battered world. Maybe I'll miss it now it's gone? Because I'm pretty sure it has gone. Something extraordinary has certainly happened anyway.

Back in my room, the grey turns to white and the white to gold. The rising sun baptises my hospital or prison chamber. It's beautiful, and the sun doesn't stop rising either. It doesn't want to. That's the thing. It just keeps on coming until the entire room's suffused in naked, healing, joyous light. I know what's happened. I know what's going on inside. The sun has risen, and it's exactly like it used to be, in the Garden of Eden – huge, colossal – five or six times its usual size. I jump up off the bed and the straps that have held me in are gone – gone altogether – like they'd never been there at all.

'Write,' he said. 'Write.' I have no pen, only my imagination. I sit on the floor, cross-legged, just to the right of the door. I close my eyes, breathe deeply and remember the angel who blew clean my soul last night. I see, in my mind's eye, a young woman sat in a café with a glass of mint tea in one hand and a little painting in the other. It's an image of a kneeling, silver-haired woman and a man clad in gold accepting her welcome, stepping down from a banner-clad ship and entering the city.

The young woman wears a red Adidas jacket with black stripes down the arms. She has close-croped hair and is very beautiful. There's music in the background. 80s pop:

When the river was deep, I didn't falter,
When the mountain was high, I still believed,

She puts down the picture and takes out her pocket-Bible. I see her name in lovely italics on the fly-leaf:

Genevieve Marie Carlton

She leafs through the book, then chooses her passage, reading slowly and meditatively. A white and ginger cat curls up on the window-sill outside and watches her read:

'Now about that time, Herod the king stretched forth his hands to vex certain of the church. And he killed James the brother of John with the sword. And because he saw it pleased the Jews, he proceeded further to take Peter also. And when he had apprehended him, he put him in prison, and delivered him to four quarternions of soldiers to keep him, intending after Easter to bring him forth to the people.

'Peter was therefore kept in prison, but prayer was made without ceasing of the church unto God for him. And when Herod would have brought him forth, the same night Peter was sleeping between two soldiers, bound with two chains, and the keepers before the door kept the prison. And behold, the angel of the Lord came upon him, and a light shined in the prison, and he smote Peter on the side, and raised him up, saying, 'Arise up quickly.' And his chains fell off from his hands. And the angel said unto him. 'Gird thyself and bind on thy sandals.' And so he did. And he saith unto him, 'Cast thy garment about thee, and follow me.' And he went out and followed him and whist not that it was true what was done by the angel but thought he saw a vision.

'When they went past the first and the second ward, they came unto the iron gate that leads into the city, which opened to them of its own accord, and they went out and passed on through one street, and forthwith the angel departed from him.'

A man walks into the café, orders a coffee and looks around for somewhere to sit. He's a biggish bloke, with a grey shaggy mane of hair, streaked here and there with splodges of both black and white. His face is full of cuts and bruises. His right arm is in a sling. He's wearing a blue serge jacket, a salmon-pink shirt, faded jeans and brown, square-toed shoes. He clocks the chair opposite Vivi.

'May I?' he enquires with a smile. Vivi gestures him to sit down, and he does.

When the valley was low, it didn't stop me, goes the song.

'Miss Carlton,' he says. 'It is an absolute joy to meet you at last. Your sister has told me so much about you. My name is DuVal, Ronnie DuVal. I'd like, if I may, to say a few words about our little community. Maybe Julie has mentioned us already? St. Mark's, our house is called. You would be most welcome, Miss Carlton, if ever you get chance, to spend a few days with us and see if our work chimes with the Divine harmonies playing so beautifully in the depths of your soul.'

The music's turned up all of a sudden and I can't hear what Vivi says, so I look at her face instead – into those wide, brown, saucer-like eyes – trying to gauge her reaction to the stranger.

I look and look again, and what I see is this – a spark, a spirit, a pin-point, a whirlwind kickstart conflagration of blazing violet light …

I knew you were waiting, 'Knew you were waiting for me.

CPSIA information can be obtained at www.ICGtesting.com
Printed in the USA
LVOW04s0115040815

448660LV00033B/2442/P